JUN 2015

THE LOST YEARS

Upon returning from their honeymoon in Tanzania, Eve Masters and her new husband David are quickly embroiled in chaos. When a hit-and-run accident almost kills them both, David develops amnesia and has no recollection of who Eve is. And then she pays a visit to his first wife — to find her dead body slumped over the kitchen table, with herself as the prime murder suspect! Will Eve be able to solve this tangled web, and will David remember her again — or will the villains win for the first time?

IRENA NIESLONY

THE LOST YEARS

Complete and Unabridged

LINFORD
Leicester

First published in Great Britain in 2018

First Linford Edition
published 2019

A catalogue record for this book is available
from the British Library.

ISBN 978–1–4448–4067–4

Published by
F. A. Thorpe (Publishing)
Anstey, Leicestershire

Set by Words & Graphics Ltd.
Anstey, Leicestershire
Printed and bound in Great Britain by
T. J. International Ltd., Padstow, Cornwall

This book is printed on acid-free paper

1

Eve Masters was bored again, despite only returning from her honeymoon in Tanzania five days previously — a honeymoon that had been packed with murder, mystery, and intrigue.

On the plane home, she had promised her new husband, David Baker, that she wouldn't get involved in any more crimes. However, she couldn't help remembering the excitement of the last three years. She knew she had a knack for private sleuthing, and if something happened again she would find it difficult to resist getting involved, despite her promise.

Eve was sitting on the beach in a secret cove near her home in Kokkino Chorio on Crete. She loved this little hideaway. Tourists didn't know about it so whenever she needed peace and quiet, she would come here with her dog, Portia. Granted, Eve didn't normally search for solitude. She liked nothing better than socialising, but there were times when even she needed to mull things over on her own.

She went into the water, wading into the beautiful clear blue Aegean Sea. She knew she was lucky to live somewhere this stunning, but she sometimes hankered after her busy life in London where she'd worked as a showbiz agent.

Glancing up towards the main road, Eve noticed a man taking photos. It looked as if he was pointing the camera at her, but she dismissed the idea. The view was spectacular so that was probably what he was interested in. She pushed him to the back of her mind and continued paddling, but when she came out of the sea she noticed he was still there — and he was staring at her.

Not one to shirk danger, and not liking being spied on, she called her dog and started running up the hill towards him. For a moment the man just stood there, but seeing two other people walking in his direction, he was off like a rocket. Eve tried to speed up, but it was a steep climb and she couldn't catch up with him.

Once she reached the main road she saw him jump into a black jeep and drive off quickly. Eve couldn't see the number plate and was annoyed with herself for not getting there sooner.

She got into her car and sat for a moment, wondering why she had chased the man. He could have hurt her or worse if the other people hadn't been there. Why was she always so rash?

Her thoughts turned to David. Should she tell him about this? She knew he would only worry, so perhaps it would be better to keep quiet. Nothing had actually happened after all.

* * *

'Darling, I'm home,' Eve shouted.

David had been an actor, but was

now a successful author, and he was writing his latest novel in the office upstairs.

'Shall I get us both a gin and tonic?'

'That would be great,' David shouted down. 'I'll just be a minute.'

Eve went to make the drinks, suddenly thinking again about the man with the jeep. She wondered if perhaps she should tell David after all? Or even Detective Chief Inspector Dimitris Kastrinakis? He had warned her against investigating crimes on numerous occasions, but this time she hadn't done anything wrong. Would he believe her?

David came into the lounge, stretching his limbs, and took Eve in his arms.

'I've missed you, darling. Did you have a nice afternoon?'

'Very pleasant,' Eve lied. David looked so happy, she couldn't spoil his mood.

'Let's sit outside,' he said. 'It's another beautiful evening. I never get tired of the weather here, do you?'

'No, it is lovely, though the winters

can be a bit too wet sometimes.'

David took Eve's hand and they sat in comfortable silence, sipping their drinks, until he spoke again.

'Well, I suppose we'd better get ready. We're meeting Annie and Pete at The Black Cat in about forty minutes.'

He'd barely touched his drink. However, David knew how meticulous Eve was with her appearance and always gave her plenty of time to apply her make-up and style her hair.

She got up, kissed David, and went upstairs. Standing in front of her mirror, she knew she had done the right thing. David hadn't guessed there was anything wrong — and it was better that way.

* * *

David decided to drive them to The Black Cat instead of walking. He wasn't bothered about drinking anything else that evening.

Eve glanced at him while he was

concentrating on the road ahead. He looked so handsome and bronzed and he sent a shiver down her spine. They complemented each other perfectly, she thought; he with his black hair and piercing blue eyes, and she with her shoulder length blonde hair, shining green eyes, and slender figure.

Although Eve was beautiful and could have her pick of men, she knew David was the best thing that had happened to her and she couldn't blow it. She assured herself for the umpteenth time that she would get used to the quiet pace of life on Crete — and keep her nose out of any mysteries that might occur.

Suddenly, they saw a car coming towards them — on their side of the road!

David honked his horn, but the car wouldn't move into the right lane. As it reached them, he swerved into an olive grove, but the other car caught his door, smashing into it. The car didn't stop, and sped away.

The air bags had deployed, but when Eve turned to David, she saw that he was unconscious. For a moment she couldn't move, but when David stirred she breathed a sigh of relief. She decided she would have to get out of the car and ring the police and ambulance, something which she didn't relish as her Greek was pretty bad.

Luckily, just as she was about to make the call, Annie and Pete drove up. Eve was relieved to have some help and waved them down. Once they had stopped, they both rushed over.

'What on earth happened?' Annie asked.

'Somebody crashed into us — and I'm sure they did it on purpose! They kept coming towards us and when they crashed into us, they didn't stop. We have get an ambulance — David's hurt!'

Pete took out his mobile and rang the emergency number. He spoke Greek very well and Eve was glad he was there to help. While he was on the phone, she and Annie went to see how David was. He was moaning with pain.

'David,' Eve cried. 'What hurts?'

'It hurts all over, but my right arm is the worst.'

'Oh David, what have I done?'

'You haven't done anything. Some idiot was on the wrong side of the road and crashed into us.'

'They did it on purpose — I'm sure of it! Someone was trying to injure or kill me and instead you're the one who got hurt.'

Annie put a comforting arm around Eve, but while she did, David pulled himself out of the car.

'David, don't!' Pete called out.

However, it was too late. Annie and Eve turned to see David collapse on the ground and hit his head. Eve quickly bent down. She felt his pulse and was relieved when she could hear his heartbeat — at least he was still alive!

Another car stopped and Betty Jones got out. Eve and Betty had never got on and Betty had even tried to destroy the budding early romance between Eve and David. She rushed over.

'Oh, David! What's happened?'

Despite hating Eve with a vengeance, Betty was very fond of David.

'Someone deliberately crashed into us — I'm sure of it. This is completely my fault,' Eve said.

'David should have never married you,' Betty snapped. 'You're quite right to blame yourself.'

Eve glared at her, but for once didn't say anything. Betty was right. Someone was after her and if David died, she'd have nobody to blame but herself.

★　★　★

Eve, Annie and Pete sat in the corridor outside the operating theatre, waiting nervously.

The ambulance hadn't taken long to arrive and Eve went with them, with Pete and Annie following in their car. Now David was in surgery — his arm had been broken.

Eve was pleased they were doing the operation straight away and hoped that, with a bit of luck, he wouldn't have to stay in hospital for too long and would soon be safely back home.

'Eve, I know it's hard, but try to keep calm,' Pete said, noticing that she was up and down like a yo-yo. 'David is in the best hands.'

'He shouldn't have been hurt.' Eve spoke angrily. 'That person in the car was after me and I wish I'd been the one injured, not David.'

'But neither of you deserve to get hurt, Eve,' Annie said.

'I do. I keep interfering in crimes that have nothing to do with me.'

'Everybody you pursued is in prison, so how could they have got to you?'

'They could have asked someone to do this on their behalf. I mean, Joanna Neonakis already did. It's possible she hasn't given up on hurting or even killing me.'

Joanna was a ruthless killer who had kidnapped David the previous year. Eve had helped to catch her, making Joanna a sworn enemy.

Eve felt like crying, but she refused to give in. Despite her promise not to get involved, she was determined to find out who had hurt her husband. She couldn't let them get away with this!

Eve was deep in her thoughts when a doctor appeared and brought her back to reality.

'How is my husband?' she asked, suddenly fearing the worst. 'I'm so worried about him.'

'Mrs Baker, your husband is fine. He will probably sleep for a few hours.'

'Thank goodness,' Eve said, not even bothering to tell the doctor that her name was Ms Masters, not Mrs Baker. 'When can I go and see him?'

'You can go down to the ward with him, but as I said, he will probably sleep for some time.'

'I want to be with him when he wakes up. You do know that he hit his head as well?'

'Yes, we will be doing tests tomorrow.

Oh, and by the way, the police are coming to the hospital, so I'm afraid you'll probably face questioning.'

'I expected as much,' Eve replied, not really wanting to see the Chief Inspector. He was bound to think she'd been up to no good.

Eve turned to speak to her friends. 'You don't have to stay. I'll be fine.'

'No!' Annie exclaimed. 'You can't stay here all night. You'll be no good to David if you're exhausted. I can bring you back in the morning — that'll be better than you driving here on your own. You've too much on your mind to concentrate.'

Eve nodded wearily. Annie was right, but she doubted she'd be able to sleep even at home.

She saw David being wheeled out of the operating theatre and she jumped up. She rushed towards him and gazed down at his bruised face. This was her fault! Betty was right; she should never have married him. All she had done was cause him angst, and now he was in hospital because of her stupidity. She resolved there and then to never pursue criminals again . . . that is after she had found out who had hurt the man she loved. He wasn't going to get away with it!

★ ★ ★

Eve, Annie and Pete sat around David's bed, watching him sleep. None of them seemed inclined to talk. Eve was still feeling guilty, still wishing it had been her who had been hurt, not David. She couldn't imagine what he would say when he woke up. Perhaps he would blame her and that would be the end of their marriage. She couldn't bear to think of life without him!

After about an hour, during which time Eve had drifted into an uneasy doze, Chief Inspector Dimitris Kastrinakis came in with another officer.

'Ms Masters,' Dimitris said.

Eve woke with a start.

'Oh, Chief Inspector, I must have

fallen asleep,' she said, straightening up in her chair.

'I'm sorry, I know this must be difficult for you, but could we have a word outside in the corridor?'

Eve looked at David, not really wanting to leave him. It would be awful if he woke up and she wasn't there. What would he think?

However, she knew she had to speak to the police, if only to make sure they realised that someone wanted to hurt her. She got up and followed the two officers in to the corridor.

'I can see you're upset, Ms Masters, but can you tell us exactly what happened?'

Eve was surprised to hear the Chief Inspector talking softly. He was usually cross with her for interfering, but this evening he was different.

'Well,' Eve began. 'David and I were driving to The Black Cat to meet our friends, Pete and Annie Davies, when suddenly a car came towards us on our side of the road. David was driving and he swerved, but the other car crashed into us and then sped away. It's all because of me.' She wrung her beautifully manicured hands.

'Now, now, Ms Masters, please calm down. What makes you think it's your fault?'

'Somebody is after me and they wouldn't be if I had listened to you and not interfered in police business.'

'So you think the car was driven towards you on purpose?'

'Of course. Isn't it obvious?'

Eve was starting to get a little prickly and the Chief Inspector noticed it.

'Stay calm, Ms Masters. All the people who might blame you for their capture are under lock and key.'

'Yes, but that doesn't mean they can't get someone to try and get rid of me.'

'I suppose you're right.' The Chief Inspector sighed, knowing this would create more work for him — and they were already short staffed.

'I suppose we'll have to question all

these people in prison. Any ideas who it might be?'

'Well, Joanna Neonakis springs to mind first. She tried it before, if you remember. I doubt if Phyllis has anything to do with this — she wouldn't have friends on the outside. But it could be anyone else I've come across. I mean, Paul Fowler never liked me. What do I do now? Sit around waiting for something else to happen?'

'I doubt if anybody will try anything again for a while after this failed attempt.'

'I'm glad you're so confident, because I'm certainly not.'

'Please try not to worry, Ms Masters. We'll put all our efforts into catching whoever did this. I don't suppose you saw what kind of car it was?'

'Well, it was black and I know it was a four wheel drive, but I didn't get the number plate as the car left the scene very quickly. There is another thing, though . . . ' Eve spoke tentatively, not knowing if she should tell the inspector.

After all, it could have been nothing. 'Earlier today, I thought someone was watching me on a secluded beach — you know, the one I was at when I found Lucy Fowler's body? When I walked towards him he ran away and jumped into a black jeep. It can't just be a coincidence, can it?'

'I don't know,' the Chief Inspector mused. 'It does give me something to think about. Perhaps you're right that someone is hounding you. At least we have something to go on — the jeep will have a dent in it so should be easier to spot.'

Eve tried to smile, but she was finding it hard. She didn't know if David would blame her when he woke up, and she was pretty certain that whoever was behind this would strike again. What's more, they would probably change cars to make it more difficult for the police to find them.

★   ★   ★

After being interviewed by the Chief Inspector, Eve went back in to the ward. David still showed no signs of waking up.

After about ten minutes, she noticed that Dimitris and his sergeant were still hovering at the door. Eve wanted to tell them to go away. David would be groggy when he woke up so she doubted he would be able to tell them anything constructive.

'How was your interview?' Annie asked.

'It was all right. I couldn't tell them much. Mind you, they're still here — no doubt waiting for David to wake up, although I'm not sure he'll have any more information for them.'

Eve went on to tell Annie and Pete about the man at the cove.

'Oh Eve, this is awful!' Annie said. 'But the police will find whoever's doing this, I'm sure.'

Eve wished she felt as optimistic.

'Mrs Davies,' the Chief Inspector said, coming back into the ward. 'Can we have a word?'

'Yes, of course,' Annie replied.

Eve wondered why they wanted to talk to Annie. She and Pete had arrived after the collision so wouldn't know much. As it was, Annie was only gone for a few minutes.

'You weren't long, Annie. What did the Chief Inspector ask you?'

'Not a lot,' Annie said, watching her husband leave the ward to talk to the police. 'He wanted to know if I'd seen anything, but of course we arrived after it happened. I suppose he hoped I had seen the black jeep escaping from the scene, but there was nothing I could tell him.'

David began to stir and Eve took his hand.

'Darling, I'm here.'

'Where am I?'

'In hospital. We were in a car crash. Don't you remember?'

'I don't think I do,' David replied, taking away his hand.

Eve was shocked that he pulled away

from her. To make matters worse, he seemed to be looking at her as if she were a complete stranger.

'You do know who I am, don't you?' she asked.

'No, I've never seen you before in my life.'

'I'm Eve — your wife! We got married about five weeks ago. Don't you remember?'

Eve was starting to panic.

'No. I'm married to a woman called Rose.'

'That was a long time ago, but you divorced.'

'Is Rose dead?'

'No, she left you for another man.'

'No, I don't believe it — not my Rose!'

David looked as if his world had fallen apart. What had happened to him?

'Who did she leave me for? I need to know!'

'It was a man called Geoff Carter,' Eve told him despondently.

'No!' he exclaimed. 'We were such good friends. I don't think I can take all this in.'

'May we speak to Mr Baker, Ms Masters?' Dimitris interrupted. Eve just sat there without moving or answering. 'Ms Masters,' Dimitris said again, this time a little sharply.

Eve looked up at the Chief Inspector.

'He doesn't recognise me. He thinks he's still married to his first wife.'

Eve was close to tears and Annie came and put an arm around her. 'It's probably just a temporary memory lapse,' she soothed.

'But what if it isn't? I could lose him!'

Annie didn't know what to say to reassure Eve — after all, she could be right. David might never remember who she was or anything about his life on Crete after Rose left him.

'Ms Masters,' Dimitris said. 'I know you're upset. However, we do need to speak to your husband — alone.'

Eve nodded and got up to leave with

Annie and Pete. She couldn't believe what was happening. Her life had been perfect, but now her world was crumbling around her!

* * *

'Mr Baker, it seems you may have lost your memory,' Dimitris Kastrinakis said. 'I'm the Detective Chief Inspector for the area you live in.'

Dimitris was sure David wouldn't remember him as they had only got to know each other when Eve arrived on the island.

'I've no idea what happened or who that woman is who says she's my wife. I feel very confused.'

'You're probably in shock, but your memory will hopefully come back soon.'

David shook his head. 'What happened to my arm?' he asked the Chief Inspector.

'You were in a car accident. Your wife says that another car drove in to you deliberately.'

'What?' David exclaimed. 'What on earth have I done to deserve that?'

'Your wife believes that whoever crashed into you was trying to injure or kill her.'

'What?' David said again, looking stunned. 'Why would anyone want to harm her?'

'Well . . . she does have a habit of trying to solve murders and mysteries. I think she fancies herself as a private detective. Some people probably blame her for them ending up in jail. I have warned her time and time again to not get involved, but she never listens.'

David shook his head again. 'I can't take this in. It's too much. My head hurts — not to mention my arm.'

'Very well, sir, I understand, but please get in touch if you remember anything — anything at all.'

David nodded and leaned back on his pillow.

This was unbelievable. There was a woman called Eve who he didn't know, but was supposed to have married. She sounded high maintenance, so he couldn't understand why he had got involved with her. He liked the quiet life and she obviously didn't. Of course she was beautiful; there was no denying that. Despite the pain and the shock he was in, he couldn't help but notice those amazing green eyes and those sensuous lips, just waiting to be kissed. Even though he couldn't remember her, he felt her pain and sadness.

However, then there was Rose. How could she have left him? He thought they were happy, but he was obviously mistaken. David closed his eyes willing sleep to come. He didn't want to be in this nightmare any more.

★ ★ ★

Eve was ready to go back to the ward when the Chief Inspector stopped her. 'I would leave him to rest for a while. He's very confused and needs peace and quiet.'

'What makes you think I'm going to

disturb him?' Eve snapped. 'I just want to sit with him.'

'David probably feels a little uncomfortable with you there,' Annie interrupted.

'But I'm his wife. I should be with him.' Eve was feeling tense and wanted everyone to stop telling her what to do.

'Look, here's the doctor. Why not speak to him?' Annie suggested.

Eve nodded and walked towards him. 'Doctor, there's something seriously wrong with my husband. He's lost his memory and he can't even remember who I am.'

'Calm down, Mrs Baker. It's probably related to the shock. There's no need to worry too much.'

'How on earth could he lose his memory?'

'He hit his head, didn't he?

'Yes. He got out of the car when we weren't looking and fell, banging his head on the Tarmac.'

'That's probably it, then. I'll go and speak to him,' the doctor said. 'You wait here, Mrs Baker. Don't worry too much. Memory loss from a head injury doesn't usually last long.'

Eve wanted to go and see David, but perhaps it was better to wait until the doctor had finished talking to him. She hoped the doctor was right and David wouldn't take long to regain his memory.

The doctor was away for just a few minutes.

'Well?' Eve asked, desperately hoping he had started to remember her.

'I'm afraid he thinks it's 2008 and believes he has just moved to Crete with his wife, a woman called Rose.'

'Oh my God. He may never remember me! I must go and see him!'

'Eve, that's not wise,' Pete said. 'He's totally confused.'

'I promise I'll only be a minute,' Eve said.

The doctor nodded and Eve rushed in.

After the doctor had disturbed him, David felt wide awake and he looked at

Eve, thinking how stressed she looked. He knew this must be as awful for her as for him.

'David, I'll only be a minute. The doctor told me I should leave you to rest.'

'I'm sorry, Eve. I can't get my head around this. I'm sure this is as upsetting for you as it is for me. The doctors are going to do tests tomorrow.'

'OK, David. I'll go for now, but I couldn't just leave without saying goodnight to you.'

She desperately wanted to throw her arms around him, but knew it wouldn't be wise. He might push her away and that would be too hard to cope with. Instead, she told him she would be back the next day.

She left the ward, tears running down her cheeks.

2

In Bandyup prison in Perth, Australia, Joanna Neonakis sat in her cell talking to Vera Ryan.

'I'm being transferred to a jail on Crete soon,' Joanna said. 'I'll miss our chats.'

'Me too. Before you go, we must come up with a plan to get rid of that Masters woman.'

Eve had inherited a house next door to Vera which Vera wanted for her son and his family. When Eve decided not to sell, Vera tried to poison her, and when this didn't work, she attempted to frighten Eve away by ransacking her house and burning down her shed.

'Sarah Marshall's out, isn't she?' Joanna remarked. 'Why don't we send her to Crete?'

Sarah had befriended Eve, but it was

just a smoke screen. In fact she was a friend of Vera's and had agreed to help her. In the end, Sarah broke Eve's arm and was sent to prison.

'What do you want her to do there?'

'Make Eve's life hell. I have friends on Crete who can help.'

'Are we going to have Eve killed?' Vera asked.

'Perhaps . . . but she should suffer for a bit first. After all, if it wasn't for her, I'd be with Charles right now. Instead he's languishing in jail and having a rotten time of it. He got a long sentence for kidnapping her, and now that Masters woman and her husband, David, are living the high life. That should have been me and Charles — and it would have been, if it wasn't for that interfering high-and-mighty busybody!'

'And I could have been seeing my grandkids every day if that Masters woman hadn't been so difficult and annoying,' Vera retorted sharply.

'Yes, she needs to be taught a lesson,'

Joanna agreed. 'Right then, let's set this plan in motion . . . '

★ ★ ★

Charles Sheffield was excited. Granted, he was in prison for kidnapping Eve Masters, but today he was being allowed a phone call to Victoria Castle in a nearby jail. Her name wasn't really Victoria, but Joanna Neonakis. He had to remember that . . . not that it made any difference — he loved her whatever her name was.

If it hadn't been for Eve, Joanna wouldn't have been captured and they would have been able to start a new life together. Charles couldn't forgive her, but he could dismiss all the crimes that Joanna had committed. He didn't care that she was a kidnapper and possibly a murderer as well.

'Joanna,' Charles said, his voice full of longing. 'It's wonderful to hear your voice. I haven't stopped thinking about you.'

Joanna's heart skipped a beat, but she knew their case was hopeless.

'Charles, I really am flattered, but we'll be in jail for a long time. There's no point in even thinking about a relationship.'

'If we follow the rules we could be out quicker. I love you, Joanna. I did from the first moment I set eyes on you. I know you feel the same — don't tell me otherwise.'

'Perhaps, but Eve Masters has ruined everything. She always does. I've been after her for a long time, but she's proved too slippery.'

'I know people, Joanna. She needs to be punished.'

'I've tried, believe me — but is it worth it, Charles?'

'Of course it's worth it. She ruined our lives and she can't get away with it.'

Joanna decided against telling him about her plans to get rid of Eve. It could all backfire and she didn't want to give Charles false hope.

'Don't give up hope, Joanna,' he said tenderly.

'You're right, Charles. I won't. Do whatever you think is best. I trust you.'

Joanna felt that the more people who were after Eve, the better — one of them had to succeed.

Charles felt happy when he put the phone down. He knew Joanna loved him, and he would find a way to punish Eve for ruining everything.

It wasn't all over — far from it. He'd be out in ten years and perhaps Joanna would agree to be his wife. It wasn't unheard-of to marry even while in jail. Then he could wait until she was released, and their life together would begin.

*   *   *

Neil Brown was relieved that he had been allowed a phone call to his brother, Gary, who was languishing in a Tanzanian jail.

Eve Masters had tried to shut down

Gary's hunting business so he'd had no choice but to kidnap her. Unfortunately that idiot of a husband of hers had managed to rescue her.

'I'm on Crete. What do you want me to do?' he asked his brother.

Neil was younger than his brother and had always been in Gary's shadow, but now it was his chance to prove himself.

'I want you to frighten that Masters woman — good and proper.'

'You don't want me to kill her, then?'

'No, not yet . . . although I haven't ruled out the possibility. To tell you the truth, I would rather do that myself. I'll probably be out in a few years and it would be something to look forward to.'

Neil was a little disappointed. He'd never killed anyone, but he wanted to prove to his brother that he could do it.

Well, instead he'd make Eve's life a misery. Gary would appreciate it and perhaps then he would take him more seriously.

3

Annie and Pete took Eve home. She was quiet during the journey and the odd tear escaped. It wasn't like her to feel defeated. She had to pull herself together and stay strong since it was going to be a difficult road ahead. All she could think about was David. She had completely forgotten that someone wanted her dead.

'Shall I get you a drink, Eve?' Pete asked when they were inside her house. He thought she could use something a bit stronger than a cup of tea.

'A brandy would go down a treat,' Eve replied. 'Help yourselves to whatever you want.'

'Would you like us to stay over?' Annie asked.

'No, it's OK — I'll be fine.'

'Somebody did try to kill you, Eve.'

'Oh — what with David losing his

memory, that had completely slipped my mind. Perhaps you should stay after all if you don't mind?'

'I'll just pop home and get us some nightclothes,' Pete said, leaving Annie to console Eve. 'In the morning I'll ring the rescue people and get them to take David's car to the garage.'

'Thank you, Pete. It would be a great help. I would rather concentrate on David at the moment, but I suppose I'll also have to think about who's after me. I don't know what to worry about most!'

'You'll have to try not to worry about either,' Annie replied. 'The doctor said David's memory loss should only be temporary, and I'm sure the police will find the person who tried to kill you. They've been competent in the past.'

'With *my* help,' Eve exclaimed. 'But neither the police nor I have got much to go on, have we? I didn't see the number plate, let alone the person behind the wheel. Anyway, I feel pretty sure they'll change cars and come after me again.'

Annie didn't know what to say. Eve was probably right; it would be difficult to catch the driver.

Eve and Annie sipped their drinks quietly, knowing there wasn't much else that either of them could say.

Suddenly there was a knock on the front door and Eve jumped. 'That can't be Pete,' she said. 'He hasn't been gone long enough — and he took a key. Let's not answer it.'

'I'm pretty sure the killer wouldn't knock at the door. I'll go and see who it is,' Annie said.

'Please be careful.'

Annie nodded. She could be wrong and perhaps the killer would get them both. As she reached the front door, she shouted out, 'Who is it?'

'It's me — Betty.'

Annie sighed with relief and opened the door.

'What can we do for you, Betty?'

'I just want to know how David is.'

'You'd better come in, then.'

Annie didn't think she could leave Betty standing on the doorstep, but she was a bit concerned about what Eve's reaction would be.

Betty followed Annie into the sitting room.

'What are you doing here?' demanded Eve. 'I'm not in the mood for an argument, Betty.'

'I only wanted to find out how David is.'

'They've fixed his broken arm, but he has some memory loss.'

'Really? What can't he remember?'

'Me.'

Eve wasn't sure, but she thought she saw a smile on Betty's lips, although she quickly pulled herself together and said, 'I am sorry, Eve.'

'He might not even recognise you.' Eve couldn't help but put in a little dig.

Betty stared at her, not knowing what to say. Finally, she asked, 'Is it all right if I visit him?'

'I'm sure it is, but as I said, he might

not recognise you.'

'He might. I've known him much longer.'

'I'm tired, Betty. Do you think you could leave?'

'There's no need to be rude. I was just being neighbourly.'

'Really? You aren't usually.'

Betty was incensed, but left, bumping into Pete on her way out.

'What did she want?' he asked Annie.

'To find out about David,' his wife replied.

'More likely to gloat over my misery,' Eve put in. 'I'm turning in, if you don't mind.' She went to kiss Annie and Pete goodnight. 'You can use the bedroom third on the right up the stairs, it's all made up ready for guests.'

'I hope you manage to get some sleep, Eve.'

Eve wearily made her way upstairs. She hoped she would feel more positive in the morning.

★ ★ ★

Eve didn't sleep much as thoughts of David filled her mind. Could their idyllic life be over so soon after they had married? She had forgotten she had been finding Crete too dull and quiet!

As the night wore on, she started to wonder if David might attempt to get in touch with Rose and try to win her back. Well, if he did, he'd have a fight on his hands, as she wasn't going to give him up that easily!

It was only in the early hours of the morning that she her thoughts turned again to the person who was trying to kill her, and she shivered despite the warmth of the night.

At about six Eve decided to get up. There was little point lying there worrying.

She got dressed and put on some make-up — whatever her mood was, she always tried to look good, and at the moment she thought it was more than necessary to apply make-up, since there were bags under her eyes and she thought she had aged ten years overnight!

She went downstairs and made herself a mug of strong black coffee, took it out onto the patio and sat down. It was already warm and she thought how lovely it would be to watch the sun rise with David next to her, holding her hand.

Would they ever do that again? She felt a tear roll down her cheek, but tried hard to stop a flood from coming. She had to remain strong for David's sake.

Eve went indoors to get her laptop. She wanted to look at their wedding photos. Perhaps if she showed them to David, he might remember her.

However, she then had an awful thought — what if David did remember everything, but wanted to leave her? After all, he did get hurt because of her. Perhaps the pain he was going through was too much for him to bear. Maybe he would think being married to someone so high-maintenance wasn't worth the trouble.

Eve's thoughts raced around as she sat there for another hour, not realising the time passing, until Annie appeared.

'Eve, you're up very early. Couldn't you sleep?'

'Not really. My mind was too active.'

'Have you had breakfast?'

'No, I don't know if I could eat anything.'

'You must try. Today might be difficult and you need to keep your strength up. How about some scrambled eggs on toast?' Annie suggested.

'OK. That sounds good,' she agreed.

Annie was right. If she was at the hospital all day, she might not get the chance to eat.

Before going to the hospital, Eve decided to take Portia for a walk. Annie had gone back upstairs, so she took her opportunity to escape since Annie would try to stop her going out on her own. Eve refused to give in to whoever was after her. She decided that a long walk was in order to clear her head.

As she walked Eve felt a little calmer. The doctor seemed to think David's memory loss was temporary, so everything should be all right. With this thought in mind, she felt more light-hearted.

However, as she walked on, she felt a shiver of fear run down her spine. She felt as if somebody was following her, but although she turned round, she didn't see anybody.

She remembered Sue Hunter, who had been stalked a couple of months previously, and she suddenly felt sick. Why on earth was she walking out on her own? Somebody was after her and she was giving them an open invitation to come and get her! Eve speeded up, wanting to get back to the safety of home as soon as possible.

As she reached her house, she noticed a police car parked outside. Fear overwhelmed her. Had something happened to David? However, she then thought that perhaps Dimitris Kastrinakis had come to check up on her.

She turned the key in the front door and went in, letting Portia off her lead to go scampering on to the back terrace. Eve followed her. Going outside, she saw the Chief Inspector sitting with Annie and Pete, drinking coffee.

'Ms Masters,' Dimitris said immediately, getting up. 'You should not be running off on your own. Someone wants you dead, so you need to be careful.'

Eve knew he was right, but she didn't like to be told what to do.

'I can't stay indoors for ever, Chief Inspector. I have to walk my dog and go shopping, and go to the hospital to see my husband.'

'If you have to go out it's better that you don't go alone,' he insisted.

'What good will that do? I was with David yesterday — and *he* ended up getting hurt.'

'Then it's probably best that you stay in.'

'I'll go crazy if I can't get out of the house.'

The Chief Inspector shook his head. Sometimes there was no talking to Eve Masters!

Eve however, was quite touched by his concern.

'However, I will try and be more cautious. I know you're only looking out for me.'

Dimitris was surprised that she was suddenly being so agreeable. Eve was usually pig-headed, but he expected she was probably scared, and upset that her husband had lost his memory. Of course, perhaps she was trying to appease him and would do what she wanted anyway.

'What do you intend to do today, Ms Masters?'

'I'm going to the hospital of course.'

'I'll drive Eve there,' Annie piped up.

'You can't do that,' Eve said quickly. 'I'll probably be there all day and I can't expect you to stay as well.'

'Don't be silly, we haven't got anything else to do. Pete can stay here and sort out David's car.'

'It is for the best,' Dimitris said.

'OK. I know when I'm beaten.'

'Well, thank you for your co-operation, Ms Masters — and please, don't do anything stupid.'

'Me?' Eve said and actually smiled for the first time since David had been hurt.

★　★　★

Eve and Annie arrived at the hospital at around ten that morning. Eve started to feel nervous as soon as they walked through the front doors.

'Annie, I've been dying to get back to see David all night, but now I'm worried. What if his memory hasn't come back yet? What if he never gets it back and doesn't want to see me any more?'

'Eve, it's early days. If he doesn't remember you now, it doesn't mean it's permanent. You need to stay calm and be patient with him. I imagine he's confused and scared, too.'

'I know you're right, but it's hard. I can't believe that this time yesterday we were out together taking Portia for a walk, and everything was fine and we were happy.'

She didn't bother to mention the fact that she was again getting bored with Crete.

'You were happy even after all you'd gone through in Africa — being kidnapped again?'

'Yes, even despite that.'

'Perhaps the events of your honeymoon are preying on your mind?'

'Not really. You know I'm good at putting things behind me. I'd never have gotten involved in all these mysteries if I'd brooded on what had happened in the past.'

'Have you told the Chief Inspector about your honeymoon?'

'Not yet. I don't know if I should bother since Gary Brown's in jail thousands of miles away.'

'But after all, you said yourself that Joanna Neonakis being in prison didn't stop her sending someone after you,' Annie reminded her.

'Yes, you're right,' Eve replied. 'Gary or Joanna could have connections outside prison.'

By this time they had reached David's ward. Eve suddenly stopped. 'I don't know if I can go in. My legs feel like jelly!'

'Come on, it'll be fine. I'll go in with you.'

Eve nodded and they both headed towards David's bed. As they reached it, David smiled, which immediately lifted Eve's mood.

'David, darling, have you remembered anything yet?' she blurted out, thinking his good mood was due to him regaining his memory.

Unfortunately, she was disappointed.

'I'm sorry, not much has come back. I do vaguely remember you, Annie, and your husband, Pete. You arrived here on Crete just after Rose and me, didn't you? We chatted occasionally in The Black Hat.'

'It's The Black Cat,' Annie said, grinning.

Eve however, wasn't able to smile.

'You still don't remember me?' she asked.

'I'm sorry, Eve, I don't. I know this must be hard for you, but it's not easy for me either.'

'I know. I'm just finding it difficult to get my head around all of this.'

Annie could see that Eve was becoming despondent again. 'It sounds like your memory is starting to come back,' she said, trying to bolster Eve's spirits as well as David's. 'I mean, you didn't recognise me yesterday.'

'You're right, of course. Everything should come back to me eventually. Annie, do you think you could leave me alone with Eve for a short while?'

'Yes, of course.'

When she had gone, David said, 'Tell me about our wedding. It may bring back some memories — and I'd love to hear about some of the mysteries you were involved in.'

Eve instantly cheered up. He was interested in his life with her and that could only be a good thing. She loved to be the centre of attention and now she had an opportunity to tell him everything that happened since they met three years ago.

However as she was telling David about their honeymoon, another woman, dark-haired and deeply tanned came in and stood by his bedside.

'Rose, what are you doing here?' David exclaimed. He wasn't sure how he felt about seeing her again.

'I heard you'd been in an accident so I came to see if you're all right.'

'Who told you?' Eve asked.

'That's irrelevant,' she said and turned back to David. 'The person also told me you'd lost your memory and thought I was still your wife.'

Eve fumed. The only person who could have told Rose was Betty — so she was trying to stir things up again!

'Yes,' David said. 'I don't remember Eve here, who is apparently now my wife, but the doctors are hopeful that I'll get my memory back.'

'Can I talk to you alone?' Rose asked. 'Things aren't going well between me and Geoff.'

'But you left me for him. I can tell you that it was a shock finding that out!'

'I think I made a mistake . . . ' Rose murmured.

'Dear God!' Eve interrupted. 'You're not married to David any more. You should leave!'

'Only if David wants me to go.'

'I don't know what I want . . . I'm sorry . . . '

Eve was so incensed she stormed out of the ward. Why did David want to talk to Rose on her own? Was he really thinking of going back to her?

Annie was standing in the corridor and decided to take Eve downstairs to the cafe for a coffee. She was hoping it might help Eve calm down, although she thought that a large gin and tonic might be more effective.

'It doesn't mean David is going to rush back to Rose, you know,' Annie said when she came back with their drinks. 'He's already remembered Pete and me, so perhaps he'll also remember Rose leaving him. That happened not long after we arrived here.'

'But what if he doesn't get the rest of his memory back? What if he thinks he's still in love with Rose? Perhaps he's already fallen in love with her all over again. Then, even if he gets the rest of his memory back, he might decide he wants to be with her, not me.'

'That's an awful lot of ifs, Eve. It's more likely that he'll remember you and all will be well.'

They both became quiet. Annie didn't know what else to say to Eve, and Eve really didn't want to talk.

Finally, Annie spoke. 'So Eve, what do you want to do with the rest of the day?'

'I honestly don't know. I want to stay with David, but he's got Rose with him now.'

'I'm surprised you stormed out. You need to get back in there and see what's going on.'

'Yes, I was stupid leaving him alone with her.'

'I'm quite happy to stay in the hospital with you all day if needs be.'

'No,' Eve replied. 'I can get a cab home later. I'm sure you have better things to do than wait here for hours on end.'

'Well, if you're sure . . . ?'

'Yes, of course,' Eve replied, taking a sip of her coffee. It was delicious. One thing that the Greeks loved was their coffee, and she had very rarely had a bad cup since coming to Crete.

★ ★ ★

After Annie left, Eve hurried back to David. She could kick herself for leaving him alone with Rose!

Entering the ward she saw Rose sitting next to David's bed, holding his hand.

She was incensed and stormed over. 'I can't believe my eyes, Rose. You come here uninvited and try to lure my husband away from me!'

'He doesn't remember you.'

'Well, you left him for another man.'

'Ladies, please. I'm not feeling too good so I don't need this fighting.'

'Sorry David,' Eve said very quickly before Rose had a chance to say anything.

Rose glared at her.

'I think you should both go. I'm tired and I'm having some more tests later today.'

Eve's heart sank. David didn't want to spend any more time with her today — but at least he wanted Rose to go as well.

'When can I come and see you?' Eve asked.

'Tomorrow, but be careful — both of you.'

'What do you mean?' Eve asked.

'I don't know. I just have a bad feeling. I had a nightmare last night that

I can't remember much about, but both of you were in it. You were screaming, Rose, and Eve, you were handcuffed. That's all I can remember.'

'Oh David,' Rose said. 'Don't be silly. It was a dream. What on earth could happen to me?'

'Quite a lot, if your partner finds out that you've been here to see David,' Eve said sharply.

'Well, I don't care,' Rose snapped back.

'Rose, please,' David said. 'I need to talk to Eve alone, just for a moment.'

Rose pouted, something she was very good at, but she left — although not before she made a show of kissing David goodbye.

Eve was angry. What right did that woman have to kiss *her* husband?

'Eve, I'm very confused. I know this must be hurting you, too, but you'll have to give me time.'

'And what about Rose?'

'I don't know. I'll be honest with you. I do seem to have feelings for her, but

I'm shocked that she left me, and that changes everything. I would never have thought that Rose was capable of having an affair.'

'We were so happy, David,' Eve said, quickly changing the subject. 'We had a beautiful wedding and then went for a fabulous honeymoon in Tanzania.'

'Was it really that good — despite the murder and you being kidnapped?'

'Yes, even with that,' Eve laughed.

David met Eve's eyes and he felt a shiver down his spine. She was a beautiful woman, but he still couldn't get Rose out of his head.

'I'll see you tomorrow then,' he said.

Eve's heart sank. She had hoped he might have changed his mind and asked her to stay a little while longer. Unusually for her, however, she decided to do as he wished.

★ ★ ★

Annie was surprised to see Eve home so soon. She was in the middle of preparing lunch, and told Eve to go and relax until it was ready.

However, Eve found it difficult to follow Annie's advice. All she could think about was how Rose had come to the hospital to see David. He was *her* husband, and she wouldn't let Rose take him away from her.

After they had all eaten, Annie and Pete went into the kitchen to do the washing-up, telling Eve to rest — they had noticed how tense she was — but when they left the dining room, Eve got up and very quietly went to the front door.

She grabbed her car keys and rushed outside. David had once pointed out Rose's house to her as they drove past it, and Eve was sure she could find it again.

However, it took her a lot longer to get there than she expected. She took a wrong turn and ended up going round in circles, which irritated her no end.

She wanted to speak to Rose as soon as possible. She needed to tell her to keep away from David and the sooner she got there, the better.

Finally, she arrived. She took a deep breath and got out of the car. Even Eve, who rarely felt nervous about anything, found that she was now wondering if she was doing the right thing. Perhaps Rose would tell David about her visit and this could easily turn him against her.

Eve walked to the front door and was about to knock when she found that the door wasn't locked. She pushed it open and shouted out.

'Rose, are you there?'

There was no reply.

Eve went in and opened a door leading to the lounge. Nobody was there. Then she went into the kitchen and saw Rose slumped over the table.

'Rose, are you all right?' she asked sharply.

There was no reply.

'Rose?'

Eve moved towards her and touched her, tried to lift her head up — and it was then that she saw the marks around her neck. She felt physically sick, but she had to know the truth. Eve felt for a pulse, but there wasn't one.

Rose was dead and it looked very much as though someone had killed her!

What was she going to do now? She knew she had to ring the police, but would they think *she* had killed Rose? Once they found out Rose was David's first wife and she had visited him in hospital, she would surely be their prime suspect.

4

Within twenty minutes, Detective Chief Inspector Dimitris Kastrinakis arrived at Rose's home. Eve had felt she had no choice but to ring the police.

'Ms Masters, how come you found the body? You always seem to be around when something like this happens.'

'I only came to talk to Rose. How could I have known she was dead?'

'How do you know this woman?

'I only met her today. She'd heard about David and came to see him.'

'How did she know him?'

Eve hesitated. Should she tell Dimitris everything? He'd find out anyway, so it would be better if she told him the truth.

'Rose is David's first wife. She turned up at the hospital when she heard that David had lost his memory.'

'I see. They're still friends?'

'No, she left him for another man — Geoff Carter, I think — but David doesn't remember her leaving him.'

'What did she want with Mr Baker?'

Eve hesitated again.

'Ms Masters, is there something you're not telling me?'

'Well, she said she wasn't happy with Geoff. I think she was trying to get back with David.'

'That's very interesting . . . '

'I didn't do it! I'm not that stupid.'

'I don't think you're stupid at all, but you have to admit that everything points to you.'

'I'm not capable of murder. Anyway, she was strangled. I'm not strong enough to do that.'

'You may be petite, but you do look as if you work out.'

Dimitris Kastrinakis studied Eve. After knowing her for three years, he couldn't believe she was a killer. Still, he had to get a statement from her.

Eve was beginning to worry. This conversation was not going her way at all, and she knew that she was being considered as a suspect — a suspected murderer! How on earth was she going to get out of this one?

'I'm afraid you'll have to come to the police station with us,' Dimitris said.

'What about my car? Oh my God, you're arresting me, aren't you?'

'Please keep calm. I just need to take a statement from you. I'll arrange for you to collect your car afterwards.'

Eve breathed a sigh of relief. They weren't arresting her, after all — all they wanted was a statement. At least for now . . .

*   *   *

Eve sat in a bare room at the police station waiting to be interviewed. How had she been so unlucky as to be the one to find Rose? Yes, she had wanted Rose out of the picture — but she didn't want her dead.

The Chief Inspector finally came in with another officer who was going to type up her statement.

'So, Ms Masters,' the Chief Inspector began. 'When did you first meet Rose Baker?'

'What?' Eve exclaimed. 'Are you saying she kept David's name?'

'Apparently so.'

Eve fumed and for a few seconds wished that she had taken David's name when they had got married. However, the feeling didn't last for long. She was an independent woman, but she was still married to David, whatever her name was.

'Ms Masters, please answer my question.'

'I'm sorry. I was just thinking. I hadn't met Rose until today. She lived a bit of a distance from us so we never bumped into her.'

'And what did she want?'

'To take David away from me. She said that her relationship with Geoff, her partner, wasn't good at the moment.'

'And what did your husband say?'

'Not a lot. He's very confused.'

'Did you follow Mrs Baker to her house?'

'No, I went home and had lunch with Annie and Pete and then drove there.'

'And you found her dead?'

'Yes. She was slumped over the kitchen table. I felt her pulse and knew then that she was dead. I rang you almost immediately.'

'Did you think of her as a rival for David's affections?'

'I don't know what I thought. I wasn't happy that she'd turned up.'

'Did Mr Baker invite her to the hospital?'

'I don't think so. He seemed as stunned as I was to see her.'

'How did she know he was in hospital?'

'News gets around quickly in such a small community. However, it could have been Betty Jones. She came over last night to find out how David was. That woman does not like me and I can well believe that she called Rose. She would do anything to split up me and David.'

'Does Mrs Baker has any relatives on Crete?'

'I have no idea. All I know was that she was living with a man called Geoff Carter.'

'Well, I think that's all for the time being, Ms Masters. Will you just sign the statement?'

'You mean I'm free to go?'

'For the time being, although we may have to speak to you again.'

Eve got up and sighed with relief that she wasn't being arrested. However, she had to find out who *had* killed Rose and why. If the police couldn't find the real killer, they might come back for her.

★ ★ ★

Once Eve returned to her car, she just sat for a while. She had no idea what to do next. Should she go to the hospital and tell David? After all, he had thought he was still married to Rose. Could she cope with him being upset at the news? Perhaps *he* would think she had killed Rose.

She needed to talk to someone else about this first — and who better than Annie? Eve knew she was dragging Annie and Pete into all her problems and she regretted it. She was usually so self-sufficient and never relied on anyone, but this time she felt she needed a little help.

Annie rushed out of the house when Eve arrived home. 'Eve, where have you been? We've been so worried we almost called the police!'

'You might as well have done, as that's where I've been.'

'Oh, my goodness! Why?'

'I went to see Rose.'

'Whatever possessed you to do that? You don't want to alienate David by arguing with her.'

'Well, as it was, I didn't argue with her. I found her slumped on the kitchen table. She's dead and I'm the number one suspect.'

'Oh no, Eve! I can't believe she's actually dead! We only saw her a few hours ago. The police can't think that you killed her. Dimitris Kastrinakis knows you so well.'

'That may be the case, but I still had to go down to the police station and give a statement.'

'But they let you go.'

'Yes, but I think they still consider me a suspect. Should I tell David about Rose?'

'Won't the police inform him?'

'I don't know. They were divorced, after all. I imagine that they'll tell Geoff.'

'I think it's best if you go back to the hospital and tell David straight out. If you don't, you'll just be worrying about it.'

'There's no time like the present, I suppose.'

'I'll come with you.'

'No, really — there's no need,' Eve said.

'Yes, there is. For a start you shouldn't really be driving in the state you're in. Plus, someone is after you, so you shouldn't go out on your own.'

'OK then.' Eve spoke wearily. 'Let's get it over and done with.'

★ ★ ★

Annie and Eve arrived at the hospital about an hour later. Eve didn't say much during the journey. She was thinking of the best way to tell David that Rose had been murdered, but there was no best way of telling him. She couldn't sugar coat this.

David saw Annie and Eve enter the ward before they saw him.

'Why are you here? I asked you and Rose to come back tomorrow.'

Eve stepped forward, knowing she didn't have any choice but to tell him about Rose.'

'I'm sorry David, but there's something we need to tell you . . . '

David thought Eve looked tired and stressed.

'Rose is dead,' she said simply.

'What?' he exclaimed. 'But she was only here this morning. How could she be dead?'

'I went to her house to talk to her about you. I saw the door had been left open and then I found her slumped over her kitchen table. She'd been strangled.'

David looked as if he was going to burst into tears. Eve was upset that he was reacting this way, but she couldn't blame him. After all, he had thought Rose was still his wife.

After a pause, David collected himself.

'Have the police been?' he asked.

'Yes. In fact, I had to make a statement.'

'They don't think it was you, do they? I know I can't remember you, but I would never have married a killer!'

Eve breathed a sigh of relief. At least

David didn't think she had murdered Rose.

'Thank you for believing in me, David.'

He tried to smile, but he was confused and scared. What was going on? Why had someone killed Rose?

'Who could the killer be, Eve? Geoff? He and Rose seemed to be having trouble. He did have a bit of a temper if I remember rightly.'

'Perhaps they had a fight and he snapped and strangled her.'

'I can't believe Geoff did it,' Annie said. 'Yes, he did have a temper, but he couldn't kill Rose. He was in love with her.'

'Who else could it be, Annie?' David asked.

'I don't know, but when she left you they moved far away enough to not socialise with any of us. We have no idea who her new friends were.'

'You said something bad was going to happen to me and Rose and it has,' Eve ventured. 'Rose is dead and I'm the prime suspect. Luckily I wasn't taken away in handcuffs, as you dreamed, but I was still taken to the police station.'

'I'm sorry. I should have done something to help both of you.'

'Don't be silly. There was nothing you could have done.'

David was feeling totally despondent. He knew he shouldn't feel like this. Rose had left him for another man, but all he could remember were the good times they had shared. Everybody became quiet and Eve wondered if they should leave David alone to grieve. However, at that precise moment the Chief Inspector came in to the ward.

'Ms Masters, everywhere I go I seem to bump into you,' he said.

'A bit of an exaggeration, Chief Inspector.'

'If you say so. I presume you came here to tell David the news?' She nodded. 'Mr Baker, I am sorry, but I'll need to question you.'

'Why? I've been here all the time.'

'I know, but we still want to know a few things.'

'I suppose you want us to leave?' Eve asked.

'If you would.'

Eve and Annie went out to the corridor to wait.

'How long ago was it that you and Mrs Baker divorced?' the Chief Inspector asked.

'Apparently it was a good eight years ago.'

'And have you seen her since?'

'I don't know. I've lost my memory.'

Dimitris felt like an idiot. Fancy asking such a stupid question! He collected himself quickly.

'How did you feel when she turned up here?'

'Confused. Eve had told me we were married and that Rose had left me for another man. After my operation, I woke up thinking of Rose and how much I wanted to see her. I felt a fool when Eve told me of the break-up of my first marriage.'

'Why, Mr Baker?'

'I told you. She had left me for another man.'

'But didn't she want to get back with you?'

'I don't know. She said she was having problems with her partner, Geoff, which was why she came to see me.'

'Was she here for long?'

'No, I asked both her and Eve to leave me alone for the rest of the day. I needed to think.'

'But Ms Masters came back.'

'She wanted to tell me about Rose rather than let anyone else break the news. I'm sure she didn't do it.'

'How would you know? You don't remember her,' the Inspector said sharply.

'I can't imagine being married to someone who could kill another person.'

'Very well, we'll leave this for now, but we'll probably be back.'

The Chief Inspector and his sergeant

walked out of the ward and nodded to Eve as he left.

Eve went back in and sat next to David while Annie went to get coffees.

'How was your interview?' Eve asked.

'I'm afraid I was a little short with the inspector. He had forgotten I'd lost my memory. I feel as if I was a bit rude.'

'Don't worry about it. He'll get over it.'

'I would imagine you know him pretty well, what with your involvement in all those crimes.'

'I do, but he's always telling me off for interfering. He's probably right. I've had some near escapes from death.'

'Then why do you do it?'

'Excitement, I suppose. And I always want to find the murderer before Dimitris does.'

'What did I think of all that?'

'You frequently asked me to stop and I have tried, but I just can't seem to keep my promise.'

'You sound like a real handful.' David grinned.

'Oh, I am,' Eve replied, smiling.

David's face was suddenly clouded with sadness.

'Are you all right?' she asked.

'I don't really know. It's been a traumatic day.'

Eve nodded. She didn't want to talk about Rose — and he didn't seem to want to either.

Annie came in with the coffees and Eve was relieved to have a break from their conversation.

'Here you are,' Annie said, handing out the drinks.

'Thanks,' David said. 'I can certainly do with one of these, though a brandy would be nice to go with it!'

'I'll try and smuggle you some in when I next come,' Eve joked.

Both David and Annie laughed.

'I suppose we should be going when we've finished our coffees,' Eve said.

She didn't want to leave her husband's side, but she didn't want to crowd him. He was trying to put a brave face on it, but his whole life had been turned inside out.

'Yes,' he said. 'I do need some time on my own to think. Just one thing, Eve . . . please be careful. I still have an awful feeling that something is going to happen to you. Try not to go anywhere on your own. I think there's more than one person after you. And above all, don't try to find Rose's killer. It's too dangerous.'

Eve shivered. David had told her and Rose to be careful and now Rose was dead. She was sure someone from her past was after her . . . but it could be anyone.

She decided to ask Annie and Pete to stay a little longer at her house. However, she couldn't promise David that she wouldn't try to find Rose's killer. She was the prime suspect, after all, and she needed to clear her name.

★　★　★

Annie and Eve arrived home. Eve had been very quiet on the journey back and Annie didn't want to intrude. She was sure Eve would speak again when she was ready.

'That was difficult, Annie,' she said at last. 'I know David was upset, although he hid it well. He's not one to show his emotions. But it's difficult to accept that he's mourning Rose.'

'I know, Eve, but once he gets his memory back these feelings will probably fade.'

'*If* he gets his memory back.'

'Hello, you two,' Pete said, coming into the lounge. 'There's a parcel here for you, Eve.'

Eve sat down to open her parcel.

'Oh my God,' she said, all the colour draining from her face. 'It's a dead sparrow!'

Pete took the box away from Eve.

'Just throw it away please, Pete.'

'No, we have to show this to the police.'

'I don't know if I can face Dimitris

Kastrinakis again today.'

'You have to, Eve. Someone is trying to frighten you and he or she must be stopped.'

It had been a horrible day and it looked as it was about to get worse. David had warned her twice to be careful — but there was nothing she could have done to stop this parcel arriving.

Eve spoke to the Chief Inspector on her phone and then said, 'He's sending his sergeant over to collect it.'

'Who on earth could do this?' Annie asked.

'I have no idea, but it's starting to frighten me. On top of everything, David is convinced that I'm in danger.'

'I can't believe he's having premonitions.'

Eve shrugged her shoulders. David had been so positive that something awful was going to happen, she had to take notice.

She made up her mind that she wouldn't go anywhere on her own any more — however difficult that might be to stick to.

5

Eve was feeling miserable, so Annie suggested that they all went to The Black Cat that evening for a meal.

'We should be safe enough if all three of us go,' Annie said.

Eve nodded, although she knew that it still might not be safe even if she was not alone. After all, David had been with her when the jeep had ploughed into them. However, Eve couldn't bear the thought of sitting at home brooding. She desperately needed a distraction.

So a little later on they were all sitting in The Black Cat. Eve was trying to make inroads into a plate of mushroom stroganoff even though she didn't have much of an appetite. She was deep in her thoughts when a woman approached her.

'Excuse me,' she said. 'The man

serving behind the bar said you might help. You are Eve Masters, aren't you?'

Eve nodded, wondering what she wanted.

'Well, there are six puppies that have been dumped outside my hotel. Nobody there wants to do anything about it.'

'It wouldn't surprise me if somebody did try and get rid of them,' Eve replied. 'I can give you the number of the rescue association, but they are always busy, they have so many puppies and kittens dumped outside the shelter.'

Eve wished she could do something to help, but knew Annie and Pete would stop her. It wouldn't be safe for her to rush around trying to save some puppies when her own life was in danger.

The woman went away and made the call.

Within minutes she was back at their table.

'They've agreed to come first thing in

the morning. I'm so relieved. They really are cute.'

'Why don't you join us?' Annie asked.

'Thank you. That would be nice.'

'How long are you here for?' Eve asked.

'A week, although I may stay longer.'

'Where are you from? I don't recognise your accent.'

'I was born in London, but we moved to the States and I picked up a bit of an accent there. I've been trying to get rid of it, but haven't managed.'

'What's your name?'

'Karen Mitchell.'

'Well, you know I'm Eve, and these are my good friends, Annie and Pete Davies.'

Karen settled down with a glass of white wine and they chatted about life on Crete. Annie and Pete praised the island, while Eve told Karen what she missed about England.

'I see a ring on your finger, Eve. Are you married?' Karen asked.

'I am, to a wonderful man called David Baker. Unfortunately, we were involved in an accident and he's lost his memory. He thinks it's 2008 — which is before I met him.'

'Oh, I am sorry. It must be difficult for you.'

'It's not easy,' Eve replied. 'However, the doctors are hopeful David will regain his memory.'

'Was the driver of the other car hurt?'

'I have no idea, but I hope so! He drove straight into us and then left the scene.'

'How awful! Perhaps the police will find them.'

'I'm not holding my breath. Oh, let's not talk about it. Let's just have another drink and relax.'

Everybody agreed and Pete went up to the bar to get the drinks.

While he was gone, Eve studied Karen. She looked to be in her mid-thirties and her very long blonde hair didn't look natural. Still, she was quite pretty. Eve thought that she looked a bit familiar, but couldn't place her.

Pete brought over their drinks and they resumed their conversation. Annie couldn't help but mention Eve's success in rooting out criminals. Eve loved the focus to be on her, so she took great pleasure in telling Karen all about the crimes that had been committed and her success in discovering the culprits more quickly than the police force.

She almost forgot her worries until she started to tell Karen about the problems surrounding her wedding day. Suddenly she stopped talking and everyone saw that she was about to burst into tears. However, she held them back and instead asked Annie if they could go home soon.

'Of course, Eve,' Annie replied. 'I hope you don't mind, Karen.'

'No, it's fine. I feel as if I've encroached on your time enough already.'

'No worries,' Eve said, pulling herself

together. 'It's been lovely meeting you, Karen. Let's do this again soon.'

They exchanged mobile numbers and before long they were in the car heading for home.

★   ★   ★

When they had all gone, Karen looked around the bar. She wanted another drink, but she didn't want to be approached by a man just because she was a woman alone. Then she noticed a girl from her hotel. They had exchanged a few words at breakfast that day. It looked as though she was alone too, so Karen decided to go over and talk to her.

'Hi, didn't we speak this morning at the hotel?'

The girl turned round and smiled broadly.

'Yes we did. Are you alone? We can get another drink and chat.'

'That's a great idea. My name's Karen.'

'I'm Liz.'

They were soon settled with glasses of wine.

'Is that an English accent?' Karen asked.

'It is. And yours too, I think, although I'm not sure what part of Britain.'

'I was born in London, but moved to the States.'

'I heard you talking to the barman about Eve Masters. Was that her who just left?'

'Yes, why?'

'I've heard she's quite an amateur sleuth.'

'Oh yes. She told me some great stories.'

'Tell me,' Liz asked, sounding excited.

Karen started recounting some of the stories Eve had told her and the two women spent an enjoyable evening talking about Eve, who would have loved what Karen had to say. According to Eve, there was nothing better than being the star of the show!

6

The following day Annie and Pete took Eve to the hospital again. She was starting to feel guilty that she was using them to ferry her around. Although they didn't complain, Eve was sure they would tire of it soon.

When they entered David's ward, he was sitting up and as soon as he saw them, he waved.

'You seem more cheerful today, David,' Eve said. 'Have you remembered anything?'

'I do have some vague memories. Wasn't I locked up in a basement at some point?'

'Yes, when you were kidnapped.'

'I also remember being on a plane, drinking champagne . . . '

'Yes, we often have a glass or two of bubbly when we fly. Am I in the picture?'

'No, I'm sorry, Eve.'

She was crestfallen. How could he not remember her while he remembered the situations?

'Don't worry about it, Eve.' David tried to reassure her. 'At least my memory is starting to come back, little by little.'

David took Eve's hand and she felt herself shiver. It was such a simple gesture, yet it spoke volumes. She assured herself that he would remember everything eventually.

'How do you feel about Rose today?' Eve asked David.

He paused for a moment, not quite knowing what to say. He was upset, yes. He still thought of her as his wife, but he had been devastated to hear that she had left him for Geoff.

'I don't know, Eve. It's been a lot to take in.'

'I understand,' Eve replied. But did she really?

She was more than a little upset that David had feelings for Rose despite the fact that she had left him. She wondered what he would have done had Rose not been murdered.

However, she knew that she had to put these thoughts to the back of her mind and concentrate on getting her husband back — not to mention solving the mystery of Rose's murder. After all she was a suspect and she refused to go to jail for a crime she hadn't committed!

Lunch appeared, looking as unappetising as usual. Annie, Pete and Eve went to the café downstairs to get something to eat, leaving David to struggle through the overcooked vegetables, the tough meat, and a roll without butter. The food in the café was miles better than the stuff the patients got. Eve decided that she would take up a croissant for David, with a cup of the delicious coffee that was served there.

When they went back upstairs, David was fast asleep so they sat waiting for a while. Then David suddenly sat up.

'What is it?' Eve asked, worried.

'I had a horrible dream . . . it felt so real.'

'What happened?'

'You were there, and you were running away from someone. It was a man, but I couldn't see his face. He caught up with you, threw you onto the ground and pulled out a gun. Then I woke up.'

Eve shivered, but she didn't let on to David that it frightened her.

'It was just a dream, David,' she said instead, trying to smile.

'I know, but it seemed real. There was someone else there who wanted to help you, but I don't know if he did or not.'

Eve didn't know what to think. Had the knock on his head causing nightmares? However, she couldn't just dismiss his dream. After all, his earlier warnings had come true . . . almost.

★　★　★

As they were driving home from the hospital, Annie and Pete left Eve to her own thoughts. Unlike Eve, they hadn't taken much heed of David's dream.

Arriving back at Eve's house, Pete dropped the two women off as he had things to do at home.

As Eve entered her sitting room, she couldn't believe the sight in front of her. There were books, papers, pictures, and ornaments strewn all over the floor!

'Annie!' Eve shouted out. 'Somebody's been here and ransacked my living room.'

Annie rushed in and gasped at the sight.

'Oh my God, this is awful! What a mess! Who on earth could have done this? Do you know if they've taken anything?'

'I don't know. The TV and hi-fi are still here. Let's look around the rest of the house.'

'We should be careful. Whoever did this might still be here,' Annie said as Eve went bounding up the stairs, taking no notice.

Annie decided to follow her despite

being wary. She waited in the corridor while Eve went through each room.

'It's the same everywhere — all my stuff is on the floor, some of it broken. I can't be sure, but nothing seems to have been taken. Of course, I'll have to check my jewellery. Mind you, I noticed something very odd. None of David's clothes have been taken out, while mine have.'

'That's weird — like you've been targeted.'

'I think you're right.' Eve looked a little frazzled.

'How on earth did they get in? I mean, you've got a burglar alarm.'

'Yes, I do . . . oh, no! With so much on my mind I forgot to switch it on before we left this morning. I can't believe how stupid I've been.'

'No, you haven't. Everything is stressful for you at the moment so it's not surprising you're forgetting things. Let's go downstairs and see if we can find where they got in.'

Eve agreed. As soon as they entered

the dining room, they saw that the patio doors had been smashed.

'I even forgot to close the shutters. What an idiot I am.' Eve was close to tears and Annie put an arm around her to comfort her.

'I'm surprised they didn't take anything,' Annie said, puzzled.

'I'm not. Whoever did this was the person who has been pursuing me. They just wanted to frighten me, or perhaps they were angry that I wasn't here and took out their frustration on my belongings. I suppose I'd better start tidying up.'

'No,' Annie exclaimed. 'The police will want to see it as it is.'

Eve sighed, not wanting to involve the police, but also knowing that she had no choice.

'You're right. I suppose I'd better call the Chief Inspector. He said to contact him if anything else happened, but I don't suppose he expected it to be quite so soon. It's a pity David hadn't predicted this, too. We might have been able to catch the person in the act.'

'Eve, please try and forget David's so-called premonitions. I'm sure they're no more than a coincidence. He never had them before, did he?'

'I suppose not,' Eve replied, not convinced.

Reluctantly she got out her mobile and made the call to the Chief Inspector. The day definitely wasn't turning out as she had planned.

* * *

Dimitris Kastrinakis wasn't far away from Eve's house when she phoned, so it wasn't long before he arrived.

'What a mess,' was the first thing he said. 'It's a good job you have Annie and Pete staying with you, otherwise they might have broken in while you were here alone and heaven knows what might have happened.'

Eve felt she could do without the Chief Inspector putting such thoughts into her mind.

'I imagine whoever did this was waiting and watching until we all went out,' she said.

'You're probably right, but you shouldn't go anywhere on your own.'

Eve was astounded. Dimitris was being particularly gentle with her. However, she didn't say anything. The chaos in her house was upsetting her too much.

'Can I clear up soon?' she asked. 'I hate my house looking such a mess.'

'No, I'm afraid not,' Dimitris replied. 'My men will have to see if there are any fingerprints and you must look to see if anything has been stolen. We'll have to take prints from you and Mr and Mrs Davies so we can eliminate you.'

'He or she is bound to have worn gloves,' Eve pointed out despondently.

'We have to explore every avenue.'

'It will take forever,' she said, agitated.

'We'll be as quick as possible.'

For once the Chief Inspector's heart

went out to Eve. She really hadn't done anything this time, yet someone was after her — not to mention that her husband didn't know who she was.

'OK,' Eve said, wanting to get this all over and done with. 'When can we go to the station to give our fingerprints?'

'How about now? You can go with my sergeant while I stay here. I'll have to call some more men in to examine the house.'

Eve nodded. She felt too deflated to say anything. She looked around the room. It was such a mess and even though she knew she could tidy it up eventually, the thought that someone had been going through her things made her cringe. It was different to the time her house in Australia had been ransacked. There was nothing of hers in that house and she hadn't felt it was her *home*.

'Come on, Eve. Let's pick up Pete on the way to the station,' Annie said.

'What about locking up the house?'

'We'll make sure it's all secure,'

Dimitris said. 'Would you like me to call someone to fix your patio doors?'

'Yes — thank you.'

'I really don't think it's safe for you to stay in this house. Perhaps Mr and Mrs Davies could put you up for a little while? Leave your car outside so it looks like you're still here.'

'What a splendid idea,' Annie said.

'Oh — are you sure?' Eve replied, not really wanting to leave her home, but knowing it was probably for the best.

As they were about to leave, Betty walked up to them. 'I saw the police car and was wondering what was going on,' she asked, looking straight at Annie, ignoring Eve.

'This is *my* house, so why don't you direct the question towards me?' Eve snapped.

'Well! There's no need to be rude. I was worried something might have happened to David.'

'He's fine. He's still in hospital,' Eve said a little more gently. 'But someone has broken into my house and ransacked it.'

'Oh, that must be horrible for you.'

'Don't pretend to care, Betty, because I know you don't,' Eve said marching straight by Betty to Annie's car.

Annie shrugged at Betty and followed Eve. She also thought Betty was probably gloating over this development.

Dimitris had watched the exchange and was worried. Eve was on edge and he hadn't seen her like this before. On top of everything, she was definitely in danger, although he didn't know exactly what her pursuer wanted. Did he just want to frighten her, or was he intending to do more?

Eve looked despondent after today's events, which wasn't surprising. He was well aware how terrible it was when someone had broken in and gone through a person's possessions. However, he knew Eve was a strong woman and she should soon bounce back.

Still, he *was* worried that she might take the law into her own hands. It wouldn't surprise him if she attempted to find out who was after her — and who had killed Rose Baker.

As Eve and Annie were getting into the car, another car drove up. A man leapt out and sprinted towards them.

'Geoff!' Annie exclaimed. 'What on earth are you doing here?'

Geoff ignored her. 'Are you Eve Masters? The woman who killed my Rose?'

Eve was shocked. 'I'm Eve, but I didn't kill her.'

'I don't believe you!'

'It's true — I just found her dead.'

'More likely murdered her! Who are you anyway? The police didn't say.'

'I'm married to David Baker.'

'Rose's ex-husband? Never! I had no idea he'd remarried. Not that it makes any difference. What were you doing at my house anyway?'

Eve hesitated. If she told him the whole story, he would definitely think that she had killed Rose, but what choice did she have?

'I'll be blunt with you. David has been injured in a car accident and lost his memory. He can only remember Rose, not me. She came to the hospital to see him, telling him she was having problems in her relationship with you. The reason I came to your house was to tell her to keep away from my husband.'

'And instead of talking, you killed her!'

He lunged at Eve, but at that moment the Chief Inspector came out of Eve's house. He rushed over and grabbed Geoff.

'Get off me!' he shouted, struggling, but he was no match for Dimitris Kastrinakis.

'What's going on here?' Dimitris asked.

'That woman killed my Rose!'

'It's more likely that *you* killed her!' Eve blurted out. 'You have as much of a motive as I have. She wanted to know if there was a possibility of rekindling her relationship with my husband. She was thinking of leaving you for David.'

'I would never kill Rose! I loved her. I can't believe she wanted to get back with David. Yes, we were having problems, but things weren't that bad.' He paused. 'But if it wasn't you . . . who else could it have been?'

'How should I know?' Eve retorted. She was getting a little fed up of this man trying to blame her for the murder of Rose Baker.

'Mr Carter,' Dimitris said firmly. 'I warn you now that I will not accept threatening behaviour towards Ms Masters. You are under suspicion as much as she is. You admitted yourself that you didn't have an alibi for the time Mrs Baker was murdered.' Geoff suddenly looked weary and despondent as the Chief Inspector went on, 'I expect you to keep away from Eve Masters — or you will be in serious trouble.'

All Geoff did was nod, and then walked slowly towards his car. Eve suddenly felt sorry for him, thinking that he must be in a terrible state after losing the woman he loved.

⋆ ⋆ ⋆

A few hours later, Eve was sitting on Annie and Pete's couch with a welcome gin and tonic. Portia lay by her feet, although she knew her dog was champing at the bit for a walk.

'I'll have to take Portia for a walk soon,' she said. 'She's been indoors all day.'

'Don't worry about it, Eve,' Pete said. 'I'll take her. Whoever crashed into you and David might still be around. They might be waiting for you to go out on your own.'

'Thanks Pete, but I can't stay indoors forever.'

She had conveniently forgotten that she had vowed not to go anywhere on her own.

'I know, but the police are onto it, so hopefully they'll catch the person who's hounding you.'

'I don't think they have much to go on.'

Before she could say anything else, the doorbell rang and Annie went to answer it. She came back a few moments later with Betty. This was all Eve needed. To see Betty once in a day was bad enough, but twice was pushing it! She didn't want to have an argument, but she also wasn't going to allow Betty to bring her down.

'Well, well, fancy seeing you here, Eve. I would have thought you'd be in the hospital with David or perhaps tidying up your messy house.'

'I was at the hospital earlier. David needs to rest because he has to have tests today.'

'How's his memory?' Betty continued, with an evil grin on her face. 'Still not remembering you?'

'He's starting to remember a few things, so I expect it won't be long before he gets his memory back completely.'

Eve thought of plenty of things she

could say to Betty, but she couldn't be bothered. She wasn't going to lower herself to Betty's level so instead she decided to talk about Rose.

'Terrible business about David's first wife, isn't it?' Eve said, looking pointedly at Betty.

'What do you mean?' Betty asked.

'She's been murdered. Didn't you know?'

All the colour drained out of Betty's face.

'What? How? Why? I can't believe this! She was my friend. I only spoke to her last night.'

'She was strangled,' Eve said simply.

Betty looked as if she were about to burst into tears. Eve almost felt sorry for her — but not quite.

'Was it you who told her about David's accident?' Eve continued.

'Me? Why would I do that?'

'Oh, to try and get them back together. You knew David had lost his memory and couldn't remember me. You no doubt hoped he would ask her to come back to him. You're spiteful, that's all I can say about you.'

'Well, you don't deserve David! He's a lovely man and *you're* ruining his life.'

'Would you like a drink, Betty?' Annie interrupted, trying to divert her attention. The conversation was becoming strained and difficult.

'A cup of tea would be nice, I suppose.'

'I'll help myself to another gin and tonic, if you don't mind,' Eve said.

Betty shook her head and rolled her eyes, and Eve nearly said something. If she wanted a gin and tonic, she could have one! However, she decided she had said enough and instead followed Annie into the kitchen.

'I'm sorry I let her in. She seems to be revelling in the fact that David doesn't remember you. Mind you, she seems genuinely upset about Rose.'

'I suppose she must have a heart somewhere. Oh, just don't tell her that I'm staying here. The news will get around the village in no time and perhaps the person who's after me will find out.'

'I won't, don't worry.'

Soon they were all sitting with their drinks. Eve was very quiet now after her earlier outburst, but after listening to Betty calling her husband 'poor David' for the umpteenth time, she exploded.

'I know you're pleased that David doesn't remember me, but he will do soon, and then you'll be laughing on the other side of your face.'

With that, Eve got up and stormed out of the room. She was about to leave and go for a walk, but then she remembered that someone was trying to kill her, not to mention the fact that she would get told off by Annie and Pete if she went out alone. Instead she went upstairs to her room.

It wasn't long before she heard Annie say goodbye to Betty, and a few moments later, there was a knock at her door.

'Come in,' Eve said rather wearily.

Annie entered.

'Don't worry, she's gone. She didn't seem to want to stay after you left. Nobody to have a go at, I suppose. Pete has just popped out with Portia.'

'That's good of him. I think Betty just wanted to revel in my misery.'

'I'm sure everything will turn out all right,' Annie said, giving Eve a big hug.

'That's the problem; I don't know if it will this time. David might never remember me.'

'Try to be positive, Eve. You've never given up on a challenge before.'

Eve paused for a moment before speaking. When she did, the spark had returned to her eyes.

'You're right, Annie. I'm not going to allow Betty to upset me any more. And another thing — I'm going to track down Rose's killer if it's the last thing I do.'

7

The following morning Eve was up early, much earlier than Annie and Pete. She was feeling more positive and felt that everybody, including the Chief Inspector, was making too much fuss.

The accident could have just been that, a plain and simple accident. However, there were David's warnings and dreams . . . but could she really take them seriously?

Eve had her usual cup of strong black coffee and then decided to take her dog for a walk. If she was lucky, she'd be back long before Annie and Pete were up, so she wouldn't get a telling off. Anyway, if somebody was after her, they would have no idea she was away from home.

As she walked along with Portia, she bumped into Kevin Fowler who was also walking a dog. Eve had found his wife's body the previous summer near the little cove where she liked to go on her own. Later Kevin got mixed up with Joanna Neonakis, but he hadn't known her true personality. Eventually he had met a lovely woman, Sue Hunter, and everything had been going well — until somebody started stalking Sue.

'Hi, Kevin. I haven't seen you since my wedding. How are you and Sue?'

The dogs greeted each other with waving tails and much sniffing.

'Oh, so-so,' Kevin said. 'Sue's gone back to England. She was having nightmares about everything that happened.'

'She will be back though, won't she?'

'She says so, but I have my doubts. Perhaps I'll go back too. I can't really make up my mind.'

'Oh, that's a pity. It seems like there are such a lot of people moving back home.'

Eve carried on with her walk, enjoying the warmth of the summer morning. For a few moments she felt as if she didn't have a care in the world. She didn't want to think about David not recognising her or who was trying to kill her.

Suddenly an arm wrapped around her from the back, and a hand covered her mouth. She tried to scream, she struggled, but couldn't get out of her attacker's grip.

'There's no point trying to escape,' a voice rasped. 'You won't get away from me that easily.'

Just as she thought all was lost, she heard the man scream, then he fell to the ground clutching his leg.

'Your damn dog just bit me!'

Eve legged it away from him as fast as she could, with Portia bounding by her side. In the distance she saw Kevin and ran towards him.

'Kevin, help me! Somebody has just attacked me, but Portia bit him.'

'Quick — we're not far from my house.'

They both ran as fast as they could,

but when Eve looked back she saw a black jeep driving towards them. So much for her attacker changing cars. Even with the danger he posed, Eve thought how sloppy he was being.

'Here we are,' Kevin shouted.

They ran into his driveway and Kevin struggled to find his key. A shot rang through the air just as Kevin opened the door. They all dived into the house, but another shot came towards them.

Eve collapsed on the floor, weak with relief that she hadn't been shot. Kevin also seemed to be unhurt. But when she looked for Portia, the dog wasn't in the house.

Eve got up and rushed back into the front garden, not even thinking that the shooter might still be lurking.

She looked around and finally saw Portia lying on the ground. All she could think of was that her worst nightmare had come true! Eve dashed towards her dog, not caring that she had hurt her leg when she had fallen.

'Portia! Oh, please don't be dead. I

love you so much,' she cried.

The dog stirred and Eve breathed a sigh of relief. However, she saw blood in her fur and started panicking again.

'Kevin,' she shouted. 'Portia's been shot!'

'Let me look,' Kevin said, coming out. He was relieved to see that his own dog was running around, agitated but unscathed. 'I think the bullet just grazed her, but we need to stop the bleeding. Stay there while I get a cloth or something.'

Eve was crying by now. If it hadn't been for her deciding to go for a walk on her own, this wouldn't have happened. Why was she always so stupid?

Kevin came back with bandages. 'The vet opens at eight, which it nearly is now. If we stop the bleeding she should be all right until then.'

He looked at Eve and gave her a quick hug. Everybody knew that she doted on her dog.

'I'm so sorry, Kevin. I shouldn't have

dragged you into this. It could be your dog lying on the ground bleeding — or even you!'

'Eve, don't think like that. If I hadn't been there you might have been the one that was shot.'

All she could think was that if her dog died, it would be her fault.

'Hadn't you better ring the police?'

'I'll have to, but my dog comes first. I have to get her to the vet as soon as possible. Oh Kevin, why did I go out alone? I'd been told to be careful and I just ignored them. I don't know who's after me, but whoever it is wants me dead.'

Kevin said nothing. He thought that if that was the advice Eve had been given, then she had indeed been reckless, but then she always was.

'Mind you,' Eve continued. 'I did manage to catch a glimpse of the man's face. He looked familiar, but I can't place him. This is the second time it's happened in the last couple of days. I met a woman in the Black Cat who I was sure I knew, but I just couldn't think who she was.'

'Don't think about it for now. Just concentrate on Portia. I think the bandage should hold until we get to the vet's. We can leave now if you like.'

'You'll take me?' Eve asked.

'Of course. You can't carry Portia there.'

'Thank you, Kevin. You've been great about all this. I don't know if I would be if you had put me in this sort of danger.'

'Of course you would. You're not one to shirk a challenge.'

Eve tried to smile, but she felt guilty for putting Kevin in the line of fire. She wasn't entirely sure about him because of his involvement with Joanna Neonakis, but he had been grateful for her help when Sue was being harassed. Kevin had probably been duped by Joanna, as had many people, so she had to give him a second chance.

★ ★ ★

Eve and Kevin returned to his house half an hour later, minus Portia. The vet was operating and told them to come back in the evening. Eve wanted to stay at the vet surgery, but Kevin convinced her that she needed to call the police.

Half an hour later, Dimitris Kastrinakis and his sergeant arrived at Kevin Fowler's house.

'Ms Masters,' he said as soon as soon as he entered the lounge. 'Haven't you been told not to venture out alone?' He sounded both angry and disappointed.

'I know. I'm sorry, but it was so early in the morning I didn't think anyone would be around.'

'If somebody is after you, they probably won't rest until they've caught you.'

Tears filled Eve's eyes, but not because she could have been killed. All that occupied her mind was her poor little Portia.

'It's all my fault that my dog's been hurt.'

'Yes, it is, Ms Masters.'

114

Eve was shocked by the Chief Inspector's response. She had expected him to console her, not to agree with her! Perhaps she really had gone one step too far this time.

'Tell me everything that happened, and slowly please. You were a little fast on the phone.'

'Well, I'm worried about my dog. I don't care about anything else.'

'Well, you need to care. Someone is out to get you and I doubt they will stop until you are dead.'

Eve tried to pull herself together. The Chief Inspector said nothing, allowing her to compose herself. Finally, she proceeded to tell him all he needed to know.

'We'll get our men onto it before he gets out of the area.'

'He's probably gone already. Perhaps you should inform the airport and the port.'

'And tell them what? We've not a lot to go on. No name, no car licence number, nothing.'

He sounded irritated and Eve knew he was still angry with her. She thought David would also be cross with her, since he had warned her to be careful, but she had ignored his advice.

'Mr Fowler,' the Chief Inspector said, turning to Kevin who had sat through all this quietly. 'I would like to speak to you alone for a few minutes.'

'Would you like a coffee?' Eve asked. 'You don't mind if I make some, do you Kevin?'

'Of course not. I could certainly do with a cup.'

When Eve went into the kitchen, her mobile rang. It was David.

'Thank goodness you're all right,' he said. 'I've had an awful feeling that something was going to happen to you.'

Eve told him what had happened that morning.

'Eve, I'm very sorry about Portia, but you really are foolish for putting yourself in so much danger all the time. If only I'd rung you earlier. I was awake at five this morning worrying.'

She was touched by his concern. Perhaps there was hope for them even if he didn't get his memory back. And perhaps she would have to take his premonitions seriously now.

His dream flashed through her mind. David had thought that a man was going to attack her — and it had happened! It couldn't just be coincidence. She was in danger and it couldn't simply be that David's mind was overactive.

'Try not to worry,' Eve said. 'I promise I won't do anything so stupid again.'

'I'm pleased to hear it. I know I don't remember you, but I do feel a strange connection to you.'

Eve was delighted by his words.

'I'm sure you will remember everything eventually, David. I feel as if I'm somewhere at the back of your mind.'

'Yes, I think you're right, although I can't explain how I feel at all.'

Hearing this, Eve felt almost light-hearted. Things would work out between them; she was sure of it. For the moment, though, she had to concentrate on finding whoever was after her.

Almost as soon as she ended the call, Eve's mobile rang yet again.

'Eve, thank goodness! We saw that Portia was missing and then I looked in your room and you weren't there! Where on earth have you been?'

'You'll be cross with me,' Eve replied and then told Annie what had happened.

'Oh Eve, why on earth would you want to put yourself in danger again?' Annie asked. 'And Portia as well. You love that dog.'

'Please don't lecture me, Annie. The Chief Inspector and David have already told me off. I definitely won't do it again, I promise. All I'm worried about now is Portia.'

'I know, Eve, but she's in the best hands. Oh, but how are you going to get back to our house?'

'I don't really know. For the moment,

I have to stay here until the police are finished.'

'Well, let me know when they are finished and I'll come and collect you.'

'Thank you, Annie. I'll see you later.'

Eve finally managed to make some coffee and brought it into the lounge. It looked as if Kevin and the Chief Inspector had finished their interview.

'David and Annie both called,' she said. 'They've told me off for going out on my own.'

'I hope you listened to them,' the Chief Inspector remarked. 'However, for now we need to focus on catching the man who's after you.'

There was silence for a while as they sipped their coffees, but then Eve spoke out excitedly.

'Oh, now I know why the man looked familiar! He's the spitting image of Gary Brown. He had me kidnapped on my honeymoon because I was trying to shut down his hunting business.'

'Ms Masters. Why didn't you tell me about this? It's important.'

Dimitris was cross again. Why did Eve keep getting in trouble, even on her honeymoon?

Eve looked sheepish. It wasn't really any of the Chief Inspector's business what had happened in Tanzania, but since she had brought trouble back with her, perhaps he needed to know.

She told Dimitris all about her honeymoon. She skipped nothing — Lawrence's murder, her kidnapping, Gary's hunting business. Now and then Dimitris shook his head. Eve frustrated him.

'That's quite a story. It could well be that Gary Brown has sent a relative after you.'

'There's no doubt about it. It shouldn't be difficult to catch him — the car has a dent in it.'

'He may change cars.'

'I would have thought he would have done that already, but he clearly hasn't,' Eve said.

The Chief Inspector's phone rang. He said very little to the person on the other end and Eve wondered if it was anything to do with the case. After he had finished the call, he turned to Eve.

'My men have found the jeep, but there's no sign of the driver. It's a rental so they're going to the hire car company to find out who rented it. He can't have got far unless he went to another company to hire another car. However, there is the possibility that he's going to try to leave the country so we will go to the airport.'

'I would imagine after all his failed attempts at getting to me, he will try to leave Crete.'

'Yes — I'm going to get going now. Please try to keep out of trouble, Ms Masters.'

She nodded earnestly. 'Of course. My main concerns at the moment are David and Portia.'

'Well, if you don't heed my warnings, you may end up dead.'

Eve knew he was right, but she didn't

want to think about the worst case scenario. There was too much happening now and she felt she had to get her priorities right. Although she didn't like it, the best thing for her to do was to leave the police to deal with the man who had attacked her.

The Chief Inspector's phone rang again.

'Really? That's very interesting. You go and ask the other car hire companies if he has rented a car. If Ms Masters had rung us earlier, we may have caught him that much easier.

'I'm going to the airport with Stavros to see if this Neil Brown is trying to get out of the country.'

'Really? You're blaming me?' Eve said, sounding incensed. 'So I should have left my dog to die, is that what you think?' She paused for a moment. 'So my attacker is called Neil Brown. Definitely a relative of Gary Brown. I knew it!'

She was stopped in her tracks by her phone ringing. She answered it and gasped in horror.

'Oh my God, no! Please tell me she's all right. I'm coming straight over there.'

'What is it, Ms Masters?' Dimitris asked.

'My dog has had a heart attack! She's hanging on, but the vet doesn't know if she'll make it.'

Eve's eyes brimmed with tears. Kevin, who'd sat quietly through the whole conversation, said, 'I'll take you to the vet right away. It is all right that I take Eve, isn't it?' he asked the Chief Inspector.

'Yes, that's fine. There's nothing else we need from either of you for the moment.'

Eve grabbed her bag and was just about to leave when the Chief Inspector said, 'I hope your dog will be all right, Ms Masters. I have a dog myself and he lives indoors, not chained up like so many dogs here.'

'Thank you, Chief Inspector.'

'Be careful. We don't know who we're

dealing with and we could be completely wrong that he might try to leave the country. He may want to finish the job he started.'

Eve nodded, then rushed to the car with Kevin.

★ ★ ★

Eve and Kevin arrived at the vet ten minutes later. She was on tenterhooks the whole journey and couldn't sit still. As soon as they got there, she jumped out of the car and rushed inside.

She went straight to the vet, even though he was with another customer. 'How is my dog?'

'Patience, Ms Masters, I am dealing with this cat at the moment.'

'I can't wait any longer to see her! Please don't tell me she's dead!'

'She's stable. You can go in and see her.'

'Thank you. I'm sorry,' she said as an afterthought to the woman who was with the cat.

Eve approached Portia slowly, feeling nervous. She was in turmoil — guilty, upset and scared. This was the second time her actions had put her dog in danger. She remembered when Portia had been poisoned by two-time killer Phyllis, not long after she had arrived on the island. It had been the first case she had been involved in, giving her a taste for sleuthing.

'Portia, my baby, how do you feel?'

The dog opened an eye. Her tail wagged feebly.

'I'm so sorry, girl, this is my fault. I promise to never put you in danger again,' she said, tears flowing down her face. Eve didn't even care that her make-up would probably be all smudged by now. All she was worried about was Portia. She was stroking her dog when the vet came in.

'She's responding well,' he said, so try not to worry too much. I'll ring you if there's any change. If she remains like this, she'll be well enough to go home tomorrow.'

'Really? That's great news.'

She gave her dog a final hug before returning to Kevin.

'How is she?' he asked.

'She's stable,' Eve said. 'I know I should look on the bright side. I usually do. I mean, even the vet is hopeful, but I just can't stop having horrible thoughts. She looked so sad lying there!'

'Come on Eve, the vet wouldn't give you hope if there wasn't any.'

'Yes, you're right. I must be positive. It's just been a bit of a hard time lately, what with the car accident and David losing his memory.'

'Yes, Betty Jones was telling me David couldn't remember you. She seemed quite happy about it.'

'I knew it was her who told Rose about David.'

'I'm sorry, I'm not with you.'

Eve proceeded to tell him about Rose's murder and how she had found her body.

'The police surely can't think it was you?'

'Oh, I'm a suspect all right, even though the Chief Inspector has known me for years now. He should know by now that I solve murders, not commit them.'

Kevin grinned. Even in adversity, Eve couldn't help but sing her own praises.

'Well, shall I take you home now, Eve?'

'I'm staying with Annie and Pete, so can you drop me off there? They're taking me to see David later this morning.'

8

Sarah Marshall spoke on her mobile. 'Well, I've seen Eve Masters, but she was with other people so I didn't have a chance to speak to her on her own.'

'What?' Vera Ryan replied, sounding shocked. 'Joanna heard that she's dead, though she doesn't know who killed her.'

'Who told her that?'

'A friend of hers on Crete. He had it on very good authority that the wife of David Baker had been murdered.'

'Well, whoever told her that got it all wrong. In fact I've just seen Eve come out of the vet's. She didn't see me, but she was with a man. There wasn't much I could do.'

'This is terrible news. I'm going to have to go. It's nearly lights-out and I must speak to Joanna.'

Vera was pleased that Joanna had got

her a mobile phone, though naturally she had to keep it a secret. She hurried out of her cell and went to see Joanna.

'You're all out of breath, Vera. Calm down. What's happened?'

Vera stood there for a few moments breathing heavily before she spoke at last. 'I hate to tell you this, Joanna, but you've been given the wrong information. Eve Masters is still alive.'

'No way! A reliable source told me that she'd been murdered.'

'That may well be, but I've just spoken to Sarah and she saw her just a couple of hours ago.'

'Who on earth was murdered, then? And who did the job anyway? I haven't sent anyone else after Eve. I was relying on Sarah to do the job.'

'What do we do now?'

'At the moment, I'm not sure. Sarah needs to find out who was actually killed. I'm going to be transferred to a jail on Crete tomorrow, so I think I'll be on top of things there. I have friends on the outside who are more than willing to help.'

'If you can, let me know how things are going.'

'Don't worry, I will. I consider you a friend, Vera, and I treat my friends with respect.'

Vera smiled and left Joanna's cell. However, the smile soon left her face. Joanna was a cold-blooded killer and she didn't trust her an inch. Vera knew she wouldn't hesitate to take down a friend if she thought they were disloyal.

* * *

Neil Brown sat on a plane at Chania airport waiting for it to take off. With each passing minute he became more and more impatient. Why was it taking so long? He thought he'd been so clever, dumping the jeep and getting a taxi to the airport. He just hoped the police wouldn't realise he intended to flee the country. He hadn't been stopped by security so the delay must be for some other reason.

He wanted to get back home to Tanzania, but he was worried what his brother would say. He was sure Gary would call him a failure, and not for the first time. Perhaps Eve Masters had been frightened by the things he did, but that wasn't enough. He had wanted to kill her.

Granted, Gary had said he was keen to do the deed himself, but he was sure his brother would still have been proud of him. However, there was no way he could stay on Crete and complete the job. Eve had seen his face, and it was now too dangerous for him.

Neil started perspiring. The plane was thirty minutes late taking off. Then he saw them.

There were two police officers marching down the aisle of the plane! Perhaps they were looking for someone else. How on earth could they have worked out that he'd be on this plane?

'Mr Neil Brown,' Dimitris said. 'We are arresting you on five counts of harassing Ms Eve Masters, and for

131

injuring Mr David Baker.'

'Me? I have no idea who those people are.'

'Don't play games with me. We found your hire car abandoned in a ditch. It had the dent in it from when you crashed into Mr Baker's car. We checked the other car hire shop in the village, but you hadn't hired a car from them. This made us realise you were planning to leave the country and had probably taken a taxi. The airport staff were very helpful in locating you. Don't forget that Ms Masters saw your face. She'll be able to identify you.'

Neil knew the game was up, but why were they were charging him with *five* counts of harassing Eve Masters? He had taken photos of her on the little beach, had driven into her husband's car, and had attacked her this morning. There was nothing else.

What was he to do? Admit his guilt, or plead not guilty and try to get away with it? What would be worse — jail in Crete or his brother's wrath back in

Tanzania? Granted Gary was in jail, but there was the rest of the family, and they wouldn't let him forget that he had failed.

Neil saw no alternative than to let the two officers lead him off the plane. He knew he couldn't run — there was nowhere to go. He got up and allowed himself to be cuffed without struggling. However, on the journey back to the police station, he refused to say anything and Dimitris knew they wouldn't be able to get much out of him.

Back at the station, Neil sat opposite Dimitris.

'I'm not saying anything without a lawyer.'

'Do you have one?' Dimitris asked.

'Not yet, but it won't take me long to find one.'

'You know that if you plead guilty, you'll probably get a lower prison sentence.' Dimitris spoke sternly.

'Do I look stupid? You can't guarantee that.'

'OK, if that's how you want to play

it, but we do have evidence. One thing I'd like to know is why you did all these things? You took photos of Eve Masters without permission, crashed into her car and injured her husband, David Baker, you ransacked her house, and then tried to shoot her this morning. And then there was the dead sparrow you mailed to her. Who set you up to do these things? Was it your brother, Gary Brown?'

'I'm not admitting anything or answering any of your questions.'

Neil wondered who had sent Eve a dead bird and ransacked her house. Clearly, there was somebody else after her and he would love to know who that person was.

Dimitris got up, frustrated, and decided that Neil Brown was going straight to a prison cell.

* * *

Neil was allowed one phone call and he decided to ring his cousin, Charles, in

Africa. They had been best friends when they were younger and Neil was almost certain that he would agree to help him out — unlike the rest of the family.

'Charles, things have gone horribly wrong. I've been caught by the police and need a good lawyer. I tried to eliminate that Masters woman, but she got away. Unfortunately she saw my face so she'll be able to identify me.'

'You know what Gary will say about this, don't you? He didn't want to give you this job, but the rest of us persuaded him. He'll never trust you with anything else again.'

'What difference will that make if I'm stuck in jail for years?'

'Hang in there,' Charles said, not really knowing what else to say. He wanted to help his cousin, but he didn't want the rest of the family turning against him as well.

'There's just one thing,' Neil continued. 'They said I ransacked Eve Masters' house and sent her a dead bird, but I didn't. From what I can deduce, she has a lot of enemies. With a bit of luck they might do the job for us.'

'Don't tell anybody about this. Eve Masters will think she's safe and become reckless. Whoever else is after her could succeed in eliminating her — not that it will count for much in Gary's eyes.'

'My lips are sealed. All I need now is for you to find me a good Greek lawyer who speaks English.'

Neil ended the call wishing he'd never come to Crete. He wasn't as tough or as clever as his brother, Gary, or his cousin, Charles. He wanted to show them that he had guts, but he had botched this job up and now he'd end up in a Greek jail. Perhaps they would transfer him to one in Tanzania, but that wouldn't be any better, especially if it was the one his brother was in.

In his office, Dimitris was feeling pleased with himself. He had no doubt that Neil Brown was guilty. He was also happy that Eve Masters was out of danger now. Despite all the trouble she had caused him over the last three years, he did have a soft spot for her.

★　★　★

Eve ended the call with Dimitris Kastrinakis and smiled. Annie and Pete looked expectant.

'Well, at least there's some good news today. The police have caught a man called Neil Brown who hired the black jeep and came after me. He was sitting on a plane hoping to leave the country when he was apprehended. He must be Gary's brother as they look so similar. He has refused to admit he did anything to me, but I'm sure there's enough evidence to convict him. After all, I did see his face and am willing to identify him.'

'That's great news,' Pete said.

'It is, as long as Gary doesn't send someone else after me. I suppose he could do, but there's no point worrying about that for a while. I feel a lot safer now so I might as well go home. Annie, Pete, it was kind of you to put me up, but I'm sure you'll enjoy having the house to yourself again.'

'But your house is a mess, Eve. We need to get it tidied up first,' Annie said. 'Plus, as you said, he might send someone else after you. Stay a little longer. You've got enough on your mind with Portia and David.'

Eve's face fell. In all the excitement, she had momentarily put both her dog and her husband to the back of her mind.

'I have to see David today, although I know he'll still be cross with me for going out alone this morning. I felt I had to be be honest with him if we want to have any chance of resurrecting our relationship. Then I have to go to the vet to see Portia. Perhaps it would be better if I stayed here for a few more days. Still, I feel safe driving myself to the hospital today.'

'I don't know about that,' Pete said.

'They've caught Neil Brown and I think it would take some time for Gary to send anyone else after me. With the evidence they've got, Gary will probably be implicated and his jail sentence increased. Thinking about it, he should be wary about doing anything else.'

'Don't underestimate criminals, Eve,' Pete said darkly. 'They hate being beaten. I know — I worked with them for long enough when I was in the police force.'

'Pete, I appreciate you looking out for me, but I really don't think I'm in danger at the moment. I need to live my life, not stay cooped up inside, never being able to go out on my own.'

'I suppose you're right, but still, I advise you to take care.'

'I will,' Eve said as she rushed out of the door.

A few moments later she returned, looking a little sheepish.

'I forgot that my car was at home.'

Annie naturally offered to give Eve a

lift back and as soon as she was there, she grabbed her car key and was on her way to the hospital.

9

Eve drove a little too fast on the highway, but she couldn't wait to see David. He had sounded so concerned about her on the phone so perhaps he was starting to remember their life together.

When she got to the hospital, she almost ran to David's ward. Reaching his bed, he looked at her and sighed with relief.

'Thank goodness you're all right. I was so worried.'

'Why? We only spoke to each other on the phone a little while ago.'

'I know, but I still have a horrible feeling that something is brewing. You're not safe, Eve, I'm pretty sure of it.'

Eve said nothing for a moment. Neil Brown had been caught so why was she still in danger? There couldn't be anyone else after her at the same time, could there? Of course David's premonitions could just be nonsense, but she couldn't completely dismiss them. After all, his previous insights had been close to the mark.

'But David, everything's all right now,' she said, trying to lighten the mood. 'They've caught the man who was after me, a relative of Gary Brown, our tour guide in Africa. He won't admit to anything, but I saw his face. There's no way he won't be convicted.'

'That is good news, but I still can't get rid of this voice in my head telling me you're in danger.'

'OK, David, I'll be more cautious. But what about you?' she asked, wanting to change the subject. 'Have you remembered anything else about us?'

'No, I'm sorry, Eve. I know it's not what you wanted to hear.'

Eve tried to smile, but with everything that had happened that day, she was finding it hard.

'Where are Annie and Pete?' David asked.

'Oh, I drove myself here.'

'You should let them help as much as possible. It's for your own good. I mean, are you sure the police have caught the right person?'

'Yes — of course.'

'Perhaps I've got it all wrong then . . .'

Eve looked at David and could see he was convinced that something else was going to happen to her. But how could she not be safe with Neil Brown in a police cell?

'I'll be fine, David — don't worry,' she said and then changed the subject again. 'Do you know when you're getting out of here?'

'Possibly tomorrow. I can't wait. The food is terrible in this hospital!'

'I know, I've been here often enough. Em . . . where are you going to stay when you get out?'

She was a little nervous of his answer.

'I don't know. Do I have a house?'

'No, you sold it and we live in my house.'

David said nothing. Eve tried to keep upbeat even though she could tell that her husband was wary of them living together again. Then she thought of a solution. It wasn't ideal, but it might get them through the next few days.

'Why don't you come and stay at Annie's and Pete's with me?' She asked.

He said nothing for a moment. He didn't want to upset her, but thought he had no choice.

'I don't know if I'm quite ready for that . . . '

'They have more than two bedrooms. I won't crowd you, I promise.'

Eve hated suggesting that they should have separate rooms, but if that was the only way he would stay in the same house as her, so be it.

'All right, then. We'll give it a go.'

Eve was relieved and took David's hand in hers. She was happy when he didn't pull away.

★ ★ ★

Eve knew she had been slightly reckless driving to the hospital both alone and a little too fast, but she was usually quite a speed machine in her Mercedes SLK. However, she knew she could be a danger on the road because her mind was preoccupied. She had to try and focus on her driving, watching her speed, and not on David and Portia. After all, the last thing she wanted was to have an accident and end up in hospital herself!

Eve kept looking in her mirror to see if she should move in for someone else to overtake. On Crete it was accepted that on the highway, cars went into the hard shoulder to allow others to pass. After a while, with most cars overtaking, she noticed a car behind her that didn't want to pass even though she pulled in.

Normally she wouldn't be bothered, but David's words came back to haunt her. He thought she was still in danger so perhaps there *was* somebody else after her. Joanna Neonakis came to mind immediately. Eve could well imagine she wouldn't give up easily.

She was relieved to reach her turning off the highway, but when she looked in the mirror, the other car was still right behind her. She thought this car looked like a Peugeot soft top, but she couldn't see the licence plate.

Eve tried to reassure herself. The turning was a popular one, so she had no reason to believe she was being followed. She told herself the car would eventually take another route and she'd have nothing to worry about. However, it kept close behind her and didn't even attempt to pass.

Eve didn't know what to do except to keep on driving. She tried to stay calm and concentrate on the road, but even when there was space to overtake, the other car stayed right behind her. She told herself it was just a nervous driver, but even as she thought this she wasn't convinced.

Eve speeded up to see if she could lose the car, but it went faster as well. She was now sure she was being followed and could feel herself getting bothered and nervous.

Suddenly Eve saw a car in front of her. Within a split second she decided to overtake it, just missing a car on the other side of the road. She sped up again, and was relieved to see that the other car hadn't managed to overtake as there were too many cars coming in the opposite direction. She knew she was near Vamos and the police station, so that was where she decided to head for.

Reaching the station, she parked up and dashed inside, just as she saw the other car come to a stop behind her Mercedes.

Eve paused for a moment before knocking at the Chief Inspector's door. She had been to this police station so many times before she felt quite at home here. However, she suspected the Chief Inspector would tell her she was imagining things. After all, they had caught Neil Brown.

'Come in,' shouted Dimitris Kastrinakis almost as soon as Eve knocked.

She opened the door, but before Dimitris could say anything else, she started talking quickly.

'Someone has just followed me from the hospital, and I managed to get away from them, but they caught up and I saw them stop just as I got out of my car to come in here!'

Dimitris got up and looked out of the window.

'Is the car still there?' he asked.

Eve looked out and saw the car leaving.

'It's just gone.'

'I don't suppose you got the number plate.'

'No, I'm sorry. All I know is that it was a Peugeot soft top. I have no doubt Neil Brown is guilty, but haven't you thought that there might be more than one person after me? David seems to think it's a possibility.'

'I suppose you mean Joanna Neo-nakis. Is she really going to keep trying to get at you? I doubt it. She'll want to get out of jail, so I imagine she'll try to keep her nose clean.'

'Perhaps you're right.'

'Are you sure you were being followed, Ms Masters?' Dimitris asked. He knew she could be given to flights of fancy.

'Of course I'm sure. The car stayed behind me the whole way from the hospital. I was driving slowly so it had plenty of opportunity to overtake.'

Dimitris didn't know what to think. It was possible there was someone else after Eve. After all, she had upset quite a few people during the last few years!

'In that case, it would be a good idea if you continue staying with Mr and Mrs Davies for the time being,' Dimitris suggested.

'They've asked me to stay a little longer and I've said yes. David has agreed to come to stay with them as well when he's released from hospital tomorrow. Being together in the same house is the best chance for our marriage.'

'Well, you should be safe there as long as you don't go anywhere alone. This must be the last time that you drive without somebody else in the car with you. I don't know what else to suggest. We don't have the resources to give you full-time protection.'

Dimitris was truly sorry about this. Despite the conflict between them, deep down he did like her and didn't want anything to happen to her.

'So Chief Inspector, has there been any progress in Rose's case?' Eve asked, wanting to know if the police still considered her a suspect. With all that had happened she had put the case to the back of her mind.

'I could ask you the same question,' Dimitris asked, a rare smile hovering on his lips. 'After all, you do seem to want to solve all my cases.'

Eve grinned, feeling a little more

cheerful. Dimitris Kastrinakis definitely knew her well!

'Am I still a suspect?'

'Well, you did have a motive, so we can't rule you out altogether.'

'I'd better get on with solving the case then before you arrest me.'

'Ms Masters, this isn't a joke,' he said more severely. 'I've told you time and time again not to interfere. And look where it's got you.'

'I know, but I'm not going to let you arrest me for something I haven't done.'

Dimitris shook his head. He knew there was nothing he could say that would stop Eve Masters. However, if she ignored his advice, she could be putting herself in even more danger. If she was right in thinking someone was still after her, she had to take care.

'Going back to the car you believe was following you . . . I don't suppose you saw the driver?'

'It's funny you should ask that. The car got up really close at one point and I'm pretty sure it was a woman.'

'Interesting. Well, be careful driving home. You have my number if you need me.'

Eve nodded, and although most of her confidence had returned, she was still a little wary as she left the police station. She made a quick dash to her car and didn't stop until she was safely at Annie and Pete's.

★　★　★

That afternoon Annie helped Eve to tidy up her ransacked house. It was such a mess and was taking a long time — it was early evening when they finished for the day.

They had made inroads downstairs, but there was still a way to go in the bedrooms. Eve felt more than a little downhearted. A few of her special ornaments had been broken and they were irreplaceable. She had discovered that her jewellery hadn't been stolen, making her think all the more that Neil Brown had just wanted to upset her.

When they got back to Annie and Pete's house, Eve started to become nervous. She had to get to the vet's soon, but was afraid of what she might find. Pete offered to come with her, as Portia would probably have to be carried to the car. For once Eve agreed. She knew it made sense, as she wouldn't be able to carry the animal on her own. The Chief Inspector's words were also in the back of her mind. She shouldn't be driving anywhere on her own — but whether she'd do as he said was another matter.

Eve had decided not to tell Annie and Pete that she thought she had been followed from the hospital. They would only stop her from going out alone and she refused to be a prisoner, despite the Chief Inspector's words.

Anyway, as the day had worn on her confidence came back and she wondered if she really had been followed . . . or was it just her overactive imagination?

However, by the time they arrived at

the vet's Eve was a bag of nerves. What if Portia had taken a turn for the worse? What if she was dead?

The vet approached her straightaway.

'Don't worry, Ms Masters, Portia's doing fine. In fact she'll be able to go home with you right now.'

'Can she walk, or do we have to carry her?'

'She'll be fine at a slow pace. Just ring me if you're worried about anything.'

Eve nodded, but knew that if she rang out of hours, there would be no reply. There were no such things as emergency vets on Crete.

Pete drove back slowly, not wanting Portia to be thrown about in the car. Eve was silent throughout the journey, stroking her pet's ears as she sat beside her in the back seat. She was still feeling guilty.

10

Joanna Neonakis was handcuffed as she was led on to the plane by two armed guards. She wasn't looking forward to the long journey. She had always travelled first class, but now she was going to have to sit in economy. To make things worse she would be in the middle seat, with a guard on either side of her. Going to the bathroom wasn't going to be easy. She supposed the female guard would go with her, and that thought was quite unpleasant. It was going to be a tedious journey.

Once the plane had taken off, Joanna leaned back in her seat, willing sleep to come, but it wouldn't. She felt claustrophobic sitting between the guards.

The same thought kept going through her mind — who had been

killed instead of Eve? Whoever it was must have some connection with David Baker.

And who had killed her? Was it someone Charles had sent to get rid of Eve? He said he was going to do something. If it was, he would be most disappointed that his plan had failed. She knew he wanted to impress her.

Still, she wasn't blaming him. He wasn't used to doing such things. He had never committed a crime before kidnapping Eve Masters. Joanna was disappointed that Sarah hadn't done anything constructive yet, but there was still time.

She looked at her guards. They were stony-faced, staring at the back of the seat in front of them. She thought they should lighten up — after all, there was no way she could escape!

Eventually Joanna fell into a restless sleep only to be woken when the meal arrived. It didn't look very appetising, but she was hungry so she ate it all.

Neither of the guards said a word throughout the entire meal. This was going to be a long flight.

★   ★   ★

Karen sat in The Black Cat nursing an almost empty glass of gin and tonic. She was feeling a little lonely and wondered if she should ring Eve Masters. After all, she had said they should keep in touch. However, Eve probably had her hands full with her husband's loss of memory, so she'd leave it for a day or two.

'Excuse me,' a voice said, disturbing her thoughts. 'I couldn't help but see you sitting here alone. Do you mind if I join you?'

Karen looked up and saw a very handsome fair-haired man smiling at her. His eyes were as turquoise as the Aegean Sea and her heart skipped a beat. However, she tried to keep herself in check. She hadn't come to Crete to meet a man.

'Is that an Australian accent I detect?'

'It is,' he said, sitting. 'Have you been there?'

'No, but I'd love to. Where do you live?'

'Sydney. It's a fantastic city. You have to visit.'

'I can imagine, it must be wonderful. Are you here on holiday?'

'Yes, and you?'

'Yes, although I'm not quite sure how long I'll be staying.'

'Me neither. I want to travel to a few more countries in Europe before I head off home. My name's Rick, by the way.'

'I'm Karen.'

'Let me get you another drink, Karen — that is, if you're not waiting for someone?'

He was finding it hard to believe that such a beautiful woman was alone.

'No, I'm not, and thank you. Another gin and tonic would go down a treat.'

Karen watched Rick wend his way to the bar and a little shiver ran down her spine. He really was very handsome and he looked as if he worked out. She had been single for a long time and she needed to put her last failed relationship behind her. Why not have a little fun while she was here?

Rick soon returned with the drinks and he smiled at Karen as he put them on the table.

'It's lovely and peaceful here, isn't it?'

'It seems to be. You'd never know there have been so many murders in the area.'

'Really? I would never have believed it. Do you know much about them?'

'A little. I made friends with a woman called Eve Masters who lives here. She's like a private sleuth and discovered the criminals before the police even caught up with them. Her stories are amazing.'

'Wasn't there a murder a couple or so days ago? I think her name was Eve as well.'

'There was another murder, but it was a woman called Rose. She was the first wife of Eve's husband, David.'

Rick was silent for a moment, then said, 'Will you be seeing her again? It would be interesting to hear about her adventures.'

'I expect so. She asked me to keep in touch. Why — would you like to meet her?'

'I wouldn't mind. I'm a writer of detective stories. It would be nice to pick her brains.'

'I'm sure I can arrange something.'

'How about lunch? They do good food here.'

'I'd love to have a meal with you, Rick.'

She was a little disconcerted that Rick was interested in meeting Eve, but then Eve was a happily married woman and he did just want to talk to her about the cases she had been involved in. No, she was pretty sure that he was interested in her — not Eve.

★   ★   ★

Eve got David settled in at Annie and Pete's. She was disappointed that he hadn't remembered their house, but it was early days.

'What would you like to do this afternoon, David?' she asked. 'I expect you'll want to have a rest first.'

'I feel like that's all I've been doing. Perhaps we should take Annie and Pete out for a meal at The Black Cat tonight, to thank them for all their help these past few days.'

'That sounds like a great idea. I'm sure they'll appreciate it. Do you fancy a coffee for now?'

David nodded, and Eve thought how upbeat he seemed. However, when she got back with the drinks, he was staring into space.

'Are you all right, David?' Eve asked.

'Yes, yes, of course. Sorry, I was miles away. I was just thinking about my novel. How on earth am I going to continue writing it? You said I was half way through it, but I won't be able to remember any of it, or my plans for the rest of it.'

'Don't be despondent. You did tell me where the book was going, so perhaps I can help. I could do the typing for you as well. I guess it will be difficult with a broken arm. First you'll need to read what you've already written. You never know, even just doing that might stir some memories.'

'Thanks, Eve. I really appreciate what you're doing for me.'

'You're my husband, so of course I'll do anything to help you.'

'But I don't even remember you. This must be as difficult for you as it is for me. I'm sure you're very frustrated with the situation.'

'It's not easy, but I love you and I'll try to take things one day at a time. Not that patience is one of my virtues. But you need to know that I'm not giving up on you, David.'

He smiled and took her hand. She shivered at his touch, but it wasn't enough. She so wished that he would kiss her and hold her close.

Pete said he would drive them to The Black Cat that evening. Eve was surprised at how excited she was to be going out. After all, they were only going to what was the equivalent of a pub, not to her favourite Italian restaurant in Chania. However, the past few days had been stressful and she just wanted to put it all behind her and concentrate on the future. A night out was a good beginning.

As well as not telling Annie and Pete that she thought she had been followed in her car, she had decided not to tell David either. They would probably all gang up on her and stop her from going out at all. She knew they only had her best interests at heart, but what could happen to her if she was with three other people?

As they sat down, they all saw Betty. She was alone and looked miserable.

'I know you and Betty don't get on,

Eve, but she looks so lost. Shall we ask her to join us?'

Eve paused. The last thing she wanted to do was to talk to Betty, but she did feel a little sorry for her. She hadn't been the same since her husband, Don, had left her.

'Oh, all right,' Eve finally said. 'I'll try to be on my best behaviour, but I can't promise.'

'What is the problem between you two, anyway?' David asked.

'Oh she didn't like me from the moment I moved to Crete. She seemed to think she was in charge of the English community over here and because I'm a forceful woman, as she is, she thought I was going to take over — even though nothing was further from my mind.'

'I vaguely remember her organising outings and dinner parties. She did like to be in control.'

'The worst thing she did, David, was try to split us up. She wanted you to date her niece, Alison.'

164

'Well, it didn't work, did it?' David said, just as Betty came and sat in the spare seat next to him.

'David, how are you?' she asked, smiling. 'It's so nice to see you out and about again. How's the memory?'

'I've remembered a few things, but not that much, I'm afraid. However, the doctors are hopeful I will eventually remember everything.'

'Have you remembered Eve, then?'

Eve bristled. Betty completely ignored her as usual, and now she was trying to stir things up.

'I'm afraid not.'

Betty smiled, irritating Eve even more.

'It doesn't mean he'll *never* remember me,' she snapped.

'Come on now, let's order our food,' Annie said, wanting to avoid a confrontation. 'I'm starving. Are you going to order something, Betty?'

'I wasn't going to eat, but I suddenly feel hungry. I can't be bothered to cook much at home. It doesn't seem worth it for just one person.'

Eve groaned inwardly. Betty was certainly looking for the sympathy vote.

While they were waiting for their meals, Annie did her best to steer the conversation away from Betty and Eve's feud. Eve had decided she wasn't going to even bother chatting to Betty and instead, she concentrated on the others.

Suddenly, David blurted out, 'Betty, you need to be careful.'

'Whatever do you mean?'

'I have an awful feeling that you're in some sort of danger. I dreamed about you last night and you were sitting in a small room — it could have been a cell — and you were terrified. Unfortunately, that's all I can remember.'

'It was only a dream,' Betty said, laughing.

'I'd take note of his dreams,' Eve put in. 'They've been coming true. He warned Rose to be careful and now she's dead.'

'Oh Eve,' Annie said. 'You can't really

believe that David is having premonitions, can you? It's all a coincidence.'

'The feelings are so strong that I can't believe they're not real,' David said, slightly annoyed at Annie's disbelief.

'I know they are,' Eve said, lightly brushing David's arm. She loved the feel of his skin, but she decided to make it brief. She was worried he might move away from her — which would surely delight Betty.

'What on earth would I be doing in a police cell, anyway?' Betty asked.

'I don't know that, I'm sorry,' David replied.

'I'd better not have another glass of wine, then. Otherwise I could be arrested for drink driving.'

Betty smiled as she said this. David was irritated by her attitude, but he said nothing more.

'Oh good,' Annie said, trying to lighten the mood. 'Here comes our food.'

She hoped this would take everyone's

minds off David and his premonitions. She couldn't understand it. David had always been so sensible.

While they ate, Betty didn't say a lot which pleased Eve no end. She wasn't in the mood for any more confrontation.

As they were finishing their meals, Karen came in with Rick. Liz followed them both in. Eve waved and they came over.

'Lovely to see you again, Karen,' Eve said. She turned her attention to Rick. 'And who's this?'

'This is Rick. We met in here at lunchtime. He's Australian — from Sydney.'

'Pleased to meet you, Rick. We went to Perth last year and thoroughly enjoyed the city.'

Liz pushed herself forward. 'I'm Liz.'

Karen was getting a bit annoyed with Liz following her around. She wanted to have at least a little more time alone with Rick. He really was gorgeous, and she was changing her mind about having a man in her life.

Perhaps a relationship wasn't such a bad idea after all. They could tour Europe together and then she could go with him to Australia. She didn't care that she had only just met him. He was too perfect to give up on!

Eve made all the introductions and then asked the newcomers to join them for a drink. She was pleased that they accepted, as Betty would be pushed right out of the limelight.

Eve noticed however, that when Pete and Rick brought over extra chairs, Betty remained rooted in her seat, making sure that nobody sat between her and David.

Having got the drinks in, David looked at Karen.

'Haven't I seen you somewhere before?'

'I don't think so. I'm good at remembering faces and I'm sure I haven't met you.'

David shrugged. He was obviously mistaken.

'Are you sure you two aren't related?' Eve said to Karen and Liz. 'You look so similar with your long blonde hair and blue eyes.'

Karen shook her head and laughed. Perhaps they were related and didn't know it.

'Karen tells me you're better at solving crimes than the police, Eve,' Rick said.

'Oh, that's a bit of an exaggeration,' Eve said, smiling with pride.

'That's not what I've heard. Can you tell me a bit about the cases you were involved in?'

Eve never tired of telling anybody about her success as a private sleuth. The rest of the evening passed with her taking centre stage, something she loved.

Betty, however, did not enjoy Eve's tales, so she went home earlier than the others.

'Before you go Betty,' Eve said. 'I'm going to have a dinner party this week and I'd like to invite you all. Will

Saturday be OK? That is, if Annie doesn't mind me using her kitchen?'

Annie was a little shocked by this as Eve hadn't asked her in advance, but didn't feel she could refuse. Eve had been through so much that it might be good for her to have something else to think about. However she was a little worried about the mess Eve would leave. Yes, she was a great cook, but she was not the tidiest person in the kitchen.

Rick, Karen and Liz all accepted the invitation.

'What about you, Betty?' Eve enquired.

'You're inviting me?' she asked incredulously.

'Why not?' Eve rather hoped it might unnerve Betty — who was surprised to be invited, but a night with David was enough for her to agree to come before she left.

'I'm shocked you invited her,' Annie said as the door closed behind Betty. 'She hasn't had a nice word to say about you since you came to Crete.'

'I'm not surprised,' David said. 'Eve has always liked to show off her cooking skills. I remember the first dinner party you held here, Eve. You went all out to impress her and it worked. Probably one of the reasons she doesn't like you.'

'You remember that?' Eve gasped.

'Good grief, Eve, I do! I can't believe it. The doctors were right. My memory *is* starting to come back.' He was as astonished as everyone else around the table.

'Do you remember anything else?'

'No, I'm afraid not, but this is still amazing progress. I've actually remembered you, Eve — so it can only get better.'

'I wish Betty had still been here. She was taking pleasure out of my misery, so happy that David couldn't remember me.'

Annie shook her head. Sometimes Eve was not a nice person at all!

* * *

On the way home, Eve asked if they could pop over to her house to pick up a few things she needed. As they got close to the house, she noticed something odd about her car. As soon as Pete stopped, she dashed out and ran over to her Mercedes, followed closely by David.

'Someone's either let down my tyres or slashed them,' Eve said, her voice trembling.

She walked around her vehicle. All the tyres were flat. David put an arm around her in an attempt to console her. For a moment she was glad this had happened, as it meant that at last she could feel her husband's arm around her!

Annie and Pete were on the scene moments later.

'Look what someone's done to my car,' Eve said, suddenly becoming quite teary.

'Oh, I'm so sorry,' Annie said. 'It's probably just kids.'

'No it isn't. Somebody is still after

me! Although I have to say, it now feels as if this person wants to upset me rather than hurt me.'

'We'd better ring the police,' David said.

'We can't call them out so late just for this,' Eve replied. 'We'll do it first thing in the morning.'

The others agreed, but insisted they all went into Eve's house just in case there had been more damage inside. However as soon as they put the lights on, they could see that nothing had changed since the day before. Eve was relieved that all the hard work she and Annie had put in tidying up hadn't been in vain.

They didn't stay long and were soon back at Annie and Pete's house, who excused themselves, saying they were tired.

'I feel like a Metaxa before I turn in, David. What about you?'

'Just a small one, thank you.'

Eve went and got them their drinks, but then she noticed that David had gone to sit in an armchair, rather than on the settee, where they could sit next to each other. She was disappointed. She had so enjoyed having his arm around her.

'I have something to admit to you, David.'

'That sounds ominous.'

Eve took a deep breath. 'I think somebody followed me from the hospital yesterday. I ended up going to the police station, but whoever it was only stopped for a minute before leaving.'

'Why didn't you tell me about this?'

He sounded quite cross.

'I thought you'd already know, what with all your premonitions,' Eve joked.

David however, didn't find it at all hilarious.

'Please, don't make fun of me.'

'I'm sorry. I didn't mean to. You've been so close to the mark with some of the things you've predicted. It's actually quite hard to come to terms with — you never had premonitions before.'

'I feel the same. I'm finding it very

strange to have such deep feelings, not to mention the dreams. I hardly ever used to remember my dreams, but now they're so vivid.'

Eve took David's hand and was delighted when he didn't pull it away. They sat in silence for a little while before David spoke again.

'I'm going to turn in now, if you don't mind. I am sorry about the car. We'll get it taken to the garage tomorrow.'

'OK. Sleep well, David.'

'Thank you. See you in the morning.'

All of a sudden Eve felt despondent. She had so hoped that David would change his mind and not use the third bedroom, but it was obvious he wasn't ready to be that close to her yet. How much longer was she going to have to wait?

11

After the police had left, Eve and David spent most of the following morning at the garage waiting for her tyres to be changed.

As they finally set off for home, Eve said, 'I think we should go and see Geoff.'

'What on earth for?'

'I want him to know that I had nothing to do with Rose's death.'

'Is it worth all the hassle, Eve? He probably won't be in the best of moods.'

'He must have come to his senses by now. Otherwise I'm sure he would have turned up at our doorstep.'

'Very well, but I'm coming with you. He's already tried to attack you once.'

Eve sighed. He was being a little too protective of her, though it was nice to know he cared about her. Perhaps he might fall in love with her all over again, even if he didn't get his memory back!

Eve drove to Geoff's slowly. She was still feeling a little nervous after her tyres being slashed. She'd hoped it was all over after Neil Brown had been arrested, but it evidently wasn't. Her life was still in danger.

Eventually they arrived at Geoff's house.

'I don't know if I can do this, Eve. I'm sorry.'

'What's wrong?'

'I still think of Rose as my wife, and to see the home she built with Geoff will be difficult.'

'Oh,' Eve said, suddenly feeling down. Rose was still in his heart despite the fact that she had left him for another man and was now dead.

'Well, you can stay here then,' Eve said, trying to hide the fact that he had hurt her deeply.

As she walked towards the door, she started to shiver despite the heat of the day. The last time she'd been here, she had found Rose's body.

Eve rang the doorbell. Nobody came to the door so she rang again. She was about to leave, feeling a little relieved, when Geoff opened the door. He looked terrible. His clothes were all crumpled and he looked as if he hadn't shaved since Rose had died.

'What do you want?' he asked gruffly.

'I'm sorry to disturb you, but I . . . oh, I don't know what I wanted. How are you, Geoff?'

'Pretty bad as if you can't tell.'

'I promise you I didn't kill Rose.'

'I never really thought you had. I mean, why would you ring the police if you'd killed her?'

'Has there been any progress in the case?'

'Not really. They can't think who would have done this, apart from me or you.'

'They really consider you to be a suspect?'

'I haven't got an alibi. I was putting

in the electrics in an unoccupied house when Rose was killed. There wasn't anyone who saw me there. I'm sure the police think I'm guilty.'

'But they haven't arrested you, so they can't have enough evidence. There must be someone else who could have killed her.'

'I don't know. She didn't have many friends, but then who knows what she got up to when I was at work? She could even have been having an affair with someone that had gone all wrong.'

'You don't really think she was having an affair, do you, Geoff?'

'I don't know what to think any more. After all she had an affair with me when she was still married to David.'

'I don't know what to say to make you feel better.'

'I've heard you've been able to solve crimes before the police. Can't you help me?'

Eve was dumbstruck. Yes, of course she'd love to solve yet another murder, but where to start with this one? The only two suspects were her and Geoff, and she certainly hadn't killed Rose!

'I'm not sure I can be any help. I don't know your circle of friends.'

'Please Eve, help me,' he pleaded pitifully.

'OK. I'll see what I can do, but I can't promise you anything.'

With that she returned back to the car.

'How did it go? You've been ages.'

'He wants me to find who really killed Rose. The police suspect him, but they haven't got any evidence. Mind you, he hasn't got an alibi.'

'You didn't say yes, did you, Eve?'

'Well . . . '

'You did! Don't you know how much danger that could put you in?'

'I did say yes, but I don't think I can help. I didn't know Rose. She could have had a whole secret life nobody knew anything about.'

'Yes, you could be right. After all, she

did have an affair when she was married to me.'

'That's just what Geoff said, but don't worry, David. There isn't much I can do.'

However, as they drove home her mind was whirring. She would like nothing better than to find Rose's killer.

★ ★ ★

On the Saturday morning Eve was flustered. She had to start preparing the meal for her guests, but she was feeling nervous. She had planned an elaborate menu, but what if everything went wrong? She would look like a fool and Betty would be over the moon! It hadn't even crossed her mind that she would be better off making a simpler meal that turned out perfect.

Eve had decided to not only have crisps and snacks to accompany the pre-dinner drinks, but she was going to make some mini spinach pies, hummus, and an aubergine dip. For the starter, everybody would be presented with a twice baked cheese soufflé, served with a rocket, parmesan, avocado and sun-dried tomato salad.

For the main course, she was going to make a beef stroganoff for the meat eaters and for herself, a timbale de riso, a rice pie stuffed with egg, mozzarella, parmesan and mushrooms. She planned to give everyone a little of her dish, always hopeful that she might convert someone to vegetarianism. Desert would be a limoncello and lemon curd cake. Everything was complicated and she knew it would take most of her day.

When she started cooking, Eve realised she was missing a couple of ingredients, so she decided to pop to the local shop. Despite it being close by, David said he would go with her.

He was feeling protective and was growing fonder of her with each day. In fact, he was more than fond of her. Every time he saw her, he felt tingly. She was definitely an exciting woman and he began to imagine being more intimate with her. However, he wasn't ready to take that step just yet. He knew Eve was frustrated with the situation, but he hoped she understood.

David and Eve decided to take Portia with them. She was growing stronger each day and Eve thought she could do with a short walk.

However, as they left the garden, Eve glanced back at her house and gasped. 'I can't believe this — look at the window!'

'What is it?' David turned to see what she was looking at and he, too, gasped. Somebody had sprayed the word KILLER on the window.

'Who could have done this?' he asked.

'I have absolutely no idea. If Geoff hadn't told me he didn't believe I was responsible for Rose's death, I would have thought it had been him, but . . . ' Eve looked as if she were about to burst in to tears. David put his good arm around her and held her for a moment.

'You'd better ring Dimitris Kastri-nakis.'

'I know I should, but I can't afford the time today. I have the dinner party to consider.'

'Eve, you have to make time. Someone is trying to upset you and goodness knows what they might do next.'

Eve reluctantly got out her phone and made the call. It wasn't long before the Chief Inspector turned up.

'Whoever did this,' Dimitris said, 'probably wanted to scare you, rather than hurt you, but that doesn't mean they won't decide to go a step further next time. My officer here will take photos and a statement.'

Eve sighed. Who had done this? It didn't seem like someone sent by Joanna Neonakis. She would do something far more frightening. However, if it wasn't Joanna, then there was someone else who hated her . . .

★ ★ ★

Eve recounted the story about her tyres and the writing on the window to her guests that evening as they sat with their pre-dinner drinks and appetisers. She wouldn't admit it, but she was now revelling in the extra attention she was getting from her friends.

'You must be worried,' Karen said. 'Especially as you thought it was all over when Neil Brown was captured.'

'I am a bit concerned, but as the Chief Inspector said, they don't seem to want to hurt me physically.'

'It doesn't mean that they won't,' Pete added.

Eve knew he was right, but she didn't particularly want to be reminded.

'Oh, let's forget about it for tonight. I've had worse done to me!'

'Yes,' David said. 'Let's enjoy our drinks and the snacks Eve prepared.'

'Did you make the pastry for these spinach pies?' Liz asked.

'Of course,' Eve replied, not blushing at all even though the pastry was shop-bought!

'I love the hummus,' Annie said.

This *was* homemade and Eve beamed with pleasure. She liked nothing better than being the centre of attention and was delighted that she was being complimented on her food.

Eve looked over at Betty, thinking how quiet she was. She saw that she was tucking into a plate full of snacks.

'Don't eat too many,' Eve said to her. 'There are three courses to come.'

'Perhaps you shouldn't have put out so much food then,' Betty snapped.

Eve was about to reply when Pete spoke, trying to defuse the situation.

'The food is too good to resist, Eve.'

Eve heard a grunt come from Betty's direction, but she ignored it. Her food was going down well, even with Betty's attitude, and the evening was turning out so much better than the day had been.

* * *

Betty remained fairly quiet throughout the meal, apart from a few words directed at David. Eve's table was round and Betty sat next to him on one side and Karen on the other. Eve had noticed how quickly Betty had dashed to get a seat next to David. The woman never changed and probably wouldn't for the rest of her days.

Eve later learned that she had been reminding David about the times they had shared over the years, leaving out any references to Eve, of course. Sadly for Betty, David couldn't remember much of what she mentioned.

When they were having coffee and liqueurs, Eve saw that Betty was looking very miserable. She did feel a little sorry for her and thought perhaps she should reach out to her, but she just couldn't. Betty had never been nice to her, so why should she bother?

All of a sudden, Betty burst into tears!

Eve looked at her in astonishment, and then tried to crack a joke.

'My food wasn't *that* bad, was it Betty?'

'How like you to be flippant!' Betty responded angrily. 'You don't know what it's like for me. I'm all alone in a foreign country because my husband divorced me for no good reason, even though I was nothing but a loving wife.'

Eve doubted that, but didn't know what to say. She didn't want to upset her even more.

Luckily Annie spoke up. 'We all feel for you, Betty, but you've been like a closed book since Don left you. We're here if you need to talk.'

'Thank you,' Betty said meekly, wiping away her tears.

Eve didn't know what to think. Was Betty genuinely that miserable or was she trying to take centre stage at her dinner party? She had only talked to David, and Eve wondered if she was trying to steal him away from her. However, it did seem a little far-fetched.

A few moments later, Betty stood up.

'I think I'll go. I don't want to ruin everyone's evening.'

'There's no need. We all understand the difficult time you've been through,' David said.

'Thank you, David. You are always so kind.'

She smiled broadly at him, annoying Eve. Betty just wouldn't give up! 'However, I will be going. I'm feeling very tired.'

'I'll show you out,' David said.

'Thank you for a lovely evening. The food was good.' Betty looked at David while she said this, not even glancing at Eve. Eve bristled, but kept quiet. She didn't want David to see her lose her temper, although it was difficult.

When David had shown Betty out, Liz turned to Eve. 'Betty doesn't like you, does she?'

'That's the understatement of the year,' Annie said, grinning. 'Betty and Eve have been at loggerheads ever since Eve arrived on the island.'

'She used to arrange events for the

English community and was afraid I'd take over,' Eve said. 'Not to mention that she's more than just a little fond of David.'

'Don't be silly, Eve,' he said.

'She's not being silly,' Pete added. 'We've always known she liked you and tonight you were the only person she talked to.'

'We all saw her gazing at you,' Rick said, laughing.

'I had absolutely no idea she liked me in that way,' David responded.

'You wouldn't,' Eve said. 'She's quite a bit older than you, and then of course there was Don, her husband. While he was on the scene, they seemed like a happily married couple. Mind you, recently you had started to get cross with her when she put me down. She's probably hoping you won't remember any of that.'

'It's very sad,' Karen said. 'Does she have any family in England she could maybe go and live with?'

'She has a niece, Alison, who is a

friend of mine. I doubt if she'd want Betty living with her.'

'We've all tried being supportive towards her,' Annie said, 'but she still seems miserable.'

'I'm trying to be nice,' Eve said, 'but I don't think she wants to be friends with me at all.'

'I was impressed with your behaviour, Eve,' David said, 'You didn't rise to her bait at all.'

Eve beamed. Things were going well. The dinner party had been a success — apart from Betty, of course — and her husband had complimented her. What more could she want?

*   *   *

When they had seen everybody out, Eve collapsed on the settee. She had told Annie and Pete that she would tidy up. Annie appreciated the gesture, although she thought she would probably have to do it all again the following day. Eve had a cleaner who came twice a week

192

and she very rarely did housework herself.

'I'm exhausted. I thought they'd never go. Their company was great, but it is almost two. How are you feeling, David?'

'Tired, but I did have a good time. At least I can sleep in tomorrow,' David said, gratefully.

'Me too,' Eve said, thinking how nice it would be to wake up next to David in the morning and not worrying about getting up.

'Rick was quiet, wasn't he?' she said.

'He was, but Karen seems to like him.'

'Liz was quiet too, although she seemed very nice. Strange that Rick came from Australia . . . '

'What are you thinking now, Eve? You can't possibly think he has anything to do with the person stalking you?'

'No. probably not. I doubt if he would tell us where he's from if he was the one after me. I'm just a bit wary, that's all.'

'I have a feeling it's a woman who's stalking you, Eve. In fact, I'm sure of it.'

'What, Karen or Liz? Why on earth would either of them want to upset me? I don't know them at all. Oh, this is hurting my head! Let's forget about it tonight and go to bed.'

'Let me help with the washing up. You can't leave it all until the morning.'

'There is a dishwasher.'

'Oh, I thought that was me!' David laughed.

Eve smiled. How she wanted to throw herself into his strong arms and feel him close to her! But she didn't want to frighten him. He would have to come to her.

'I had better let Portia out before bed.'

'I'll go up then,' David said moving closer.

She could feel her heart beating and her hopes for a night with David grew. However, he just lightly brushed his lips against hers, frustrating her again.

At that point, she felt like initiating

romance and to hell with the consequences, but at the last moment she held back. It wasn't the right time, David wasn't ready.

Eve didn't rush straight off to bed in the end. She poured herself a small Metaxa and sat for a while outside in the warm summer air, thinking.

When she finally went to bed, she couldn't sleep, despite her tiredness.

What she didn't realise was that David too was having trouble sleeping. All he could think about was Eve. He was falling in love with her all over again and he didn't need to get his memory back to realise it.

12

Eve got up early again the following day. She was tired, but just couldn't sleep. She wished she could go for a pleasant walk with her dog. Portia was ready to be taken out for short walks. However, she decided not to risk it as David, Annie and Pete would be cross with her and she didn't want to upset them, especially not David.

David emerged not long after Eve and she noticed how drained he looked.

'Are you all right? You don't seem yourself.'

'Oh, I had trouble sleeping and then when I finally dropped off I had another unsettling dream. I don't know if I should tell you about it . . . '

'You have to now that you've mentioned it. You can't keep me in suspense.'

'Well . . . Joanna Neonakis was in the

dream. She was chasing you and when she caught you she tried to strangle you! Then I woke up.'

Eve breathed a sigh of relief.

'Joanna's in jail, David. There's no way she can get to me.' She was certain this was one premonition that couldn't come true.

'Well, I hope I'm wrong then. Of course, it could mean she's sending someone after you rather than doing the deed herself.'

'I said I'd be careful and not go out on my own, so what chance has she got?'

'Very little I suppose,' David replied, but he didn't sound convinced.

He took her hand and Eve smiled, forgetting his words. His touch was electric and she longed for more.

Their intimate moment was interrupted by Annie and Pete coming down for breakfast. They suggested they go to The Black Cat for dinner as Eve had worked so hard the previous day. They thought she had earned a reward.

Later that day, Eve was enjoying quiche in The Black Cat when her mobile rang. She didn't always pick up when she was with other people as she felt it was rude, but when she saw it was the Chief Inspector, she thought she should answer.

'Chief Inspector, what can I do for you?'

'I have some bad news,' he replied. 'Joanna Neonakis has escaped while being transferred from Australia to a prison here on Crete. There were two guards escorting her, but she had her escape planned. Her men overpowered the guards and now she's on the run. I don't think she'll get far, but you need to be careful.'

'Thank you for letting me know,' Eve said, her hands starting to shake as she ended the call.

'What is it, Eve? You look white as a sheet,' David asked, concerned.

'Joanna Neonakis has escaped. She

was being brought over to a Cretan jail and her guards were caught unawares by her men.'

'She's on the run here on Crete?' Annie asked.

'Yes, I'm afraid so. Oh, David, perhaps your dream will come true after all!'

'We'd better get back home,' David said.

'I'm sure she won't try anything while I'm here with all of you.'

'I reckon that we're safe here,' Annie put in.

'But I had another dream,' David told Pete and Annie. 'I dreamed Eve was being strangled by Joanna, and I can't just dismiss it.'

'David,' Pete said. 'I know you think your dreams come true, but they are only dreams.'

'Yes, I know, but I've been right on the mark a few times already.'

'It can't just be coincidence,' Eve said. 'And I have to take heed of warnings from the Chief Inspector.'

'Whether or not Joanna is after you, you'd be best not going anywhere on your own,' Pete said.

Eve nodded and then looked at David. He looked strained, and all she wanted to do was wrap her arms around him and tell him it was going to be all right . . . but would it?

* * *

On the way back to Annie and Pete's, Eve asked if she could just pop back to her house to collect the post. She wished she was going back home for good and taking David with her. Perhaps if they were alone together, more progress might be made in their relationship. However, she knew she was probably safer at Annie and Pete's, especially after the latest development.

Arriving at her house, David said he was going in with her. He realised how desperately he wanted to keep her safe and was shocked how deep his feelings had become for this woman he barely remembered.

Although she wouldn't admit it, Eve was pleased he was coming in with her. She liked to appear tough, but she didn't feel brave at the moment. Joanna's escape had hit her hard, especially after hearing about David's dream.

As they entered the house, Eve picked up the post. There wasn't much — a couple of bills and a letter. She noticed there wasn't a stamp on the letter and felt a shiver of fear running down her spine. She ripped it open and gasped.

It read simply, *I WILL DESTROY YOU*.

'Are you all right, Eve?' David asked.

She said nothing, just pushed the letter into his hands.

'Oh, Eve, I'm so sorry. Whoever this is just won't give up.'

'I thought it was all over when Neil Brown was caught, but will it ever end?'

'Come on, let's lock up the house

and get back to Annie and Pete's. We'll have to let the Chief Inspector see the letter.'

'No. I can't bother him again, David.'

He shook his head. Sometimes Eve could be so pig-headed!

'It must be Joanna,' she finally said. 'In fact I'm almost certain it's her. Your dreams have all come true in one way or another. I wouldn't have thought she would do anything so petty as sending an anonymous letter, but I think she's just doing little things to spook me until the main event when she'll try to kill me!

'But she won't — I won't let her! I've been a match for her in the past, and this is no different.'

'Oh Eve, please don't get involved. Leave it to the police. You need to keep out of the limelight and stick with me.'

He put his arm around her and for a moment she thought that just maybe all these threats were worthwhile if they brought her husband back to her.

Getting back in the car, Eve told Annie and Pete about the letter.

'You must tell the Chief Inspector,' Pete said.

'Must I? He'll be getting fed up of me.'

'I think he's already fed up of you, Eve,' Annie said, grinning. She had tried to lighten the mood but her efforts weren't successful.

'Pete's right,' agreed David. 'He'll be cross with you if you don't tell him. I mean, there could be fingerprints on the letter.'

'I doubt it. If Joanna is behind all of this she'll have been careful,' Eve said.

'We'll head to the station now,' Pete said.

Eve sighed. She was getting fed up of going there. All she wanted was a bit of peace and quiet. At this moment she refused to acknowledge that a quiet life would never suit her!

Arriving at the police station, they all

got out of the car. Eve wished they would just let her get on with it. She felt claustrophobic and needed to do this on her own, but the others wouldn't let her.

Entering the police station, Eve saw Stavros, the Chief Inspector's assistant.

'Ms Masters, the Chief Inspector has gone home for the night. Can I help you?'

'I received an anonymous letter today.'

'Let me see it.'

Eve handed the letter to Stavros.

'Well, this isn't good at all. I'll show it to my boss when he comes to work in the morning.'

Eve nodded and everyone traipsed out of the station again. Eve felt like she was like a prisoner with three guards not letting her go anywhere!

The sooner Dimitris solved this case the better. She had barely had time to try and get to the bottom of Rose's murder, and the way things were going, she wouldn't be able to do anything anyway. Annie, Pete and David were all watching her like a hawk.

13

The following day, Eve was restless. Everybody was reading, but she couldn't concentrate on her book. She felt trapped and wanted to escape.

'I have to walk my dog,' she said suddenly.

'No you don't,' Pete replied. 'It's better if you stay here. I'll walk her for you.'

'I don't care what anyone says, I'm going, so just try and stop me!'

With that, she jumped up and was in the hall in no time — but closely followed by the others.

'Eve, wait,' David said. 'I'm coming with you.'

'If you want to, you can come, but I warn you, I'm not in the mood for chatting.'

She put on her walking shoes, grabbed Portia, and opened the front door.

'Eve, please,' David said. 'We're only trying to look after you.'

'I know.' Eve sighed, feeling a little guilty. All three of them wanted to protect her and she was stupid, acting like this. 'I'm sorry,' she said.

Saying sorry didn't come easily for Eve, so they all knew she was being genuine.

'OK then, why don't we *all* take Portia for a walk?' Eve asked.

'That seems like a good idea,' Pete replied. 'Safety in numbers.

Eve nodded, but still wished she could go out on her own.

     *   *   *

That evening, they all went to The Black Cat for a drink. It hadn't been planned, but everybody was worried about Eve. She had been so restless all day and they were worried she might do something rash to alleviate her boredom. Nothing untoward had happened on their walk, and Eve had been

207

relieved. If it had, she'd probably never be able to go out again — or at least not until her pursuer had been caught.

In the bar, Eve noticed Rick and Karen chatting in a corner. There was no sign of Liz anywhere. She thought that perhaps Liz had realised she was a spare wheel. In another corner, there was Betty nursing a glass of wine.

'What do you say, Eve? Shall we invite Betty over?' Annie asked.

'If that's want you want, that's fine. I don't care either way, but don't expect me to be nice to her.'

'All right, I'll ask her.'

Annie couldn't believe it. One moment Eve was remorseful, the next she was being awkward. She knew she should be used to it by now, but it still grated when Eve was in this sort of a mood. However, she had to forgive her. Eve was under so much strain at the moment. Annie wondered how she would act if someone was trying to kill her and her husband didn't remember her.

It wasn't long before Betty settled with the group. 'I'll just have one drink,' she said. 'I had such a late night at your dinner party, David, and it's taken its toll on me.'

Eve bristled. It had been *her* dinner party; she had done all the work, but Betty wouldn't acknowledge it. However, at least if Betty was only having one drink, she wouldn't have much time to criticise her, and indeed it wasn't that long before Betty finished her wine and left. She hadn't directed one question at Eve, although she had spoken to David. Somehow she had managed to grab the chair next to him as usual.

Once Betty left, Rick and Karen came over and asked if they could join them. Eve wondered if they didn't like Betty either. Everybody was fine about Rick and Karen joining them and it wasn't long before Eve took centre stage and told them about the anonymous letter.

'Are the police looking into it?' Rick

asked. 'You must feel like you're looking over your shoulder all the time.'

'I do a bit, but I feel safe with David,' she said, looking over at him and smiling. 'However, there is something else . . . You remember I told you about Joanna Neonakis? Well, she was being brought to a jail here on Crete, but she escaped. She's on the loose and could be after me! Although I don't think an anonymous letter is her style — but if it wasn't her, who else could it be?'

'Anybody could have it in for you,' David said. 'That's why we're all so worried and didn't let you go out on your own this morning.'

'I know you're all just concerned about me, but I can't help feeling trapped.'

'It's for your own good,' Pete said.

Eve didn't like being told what to do, even if she got sensible advice. However, she smiled sweetly and took David's hand. She was relieved when he didn't take it away. However, it wasn't long before he started nodding off.

'I think we need to go soon. David's tired.'

'Of course,' Annie said.

'It's been lovely seeing you again,' Karen said. 'We must meet up again before we leave.'

'That would be nice,' David said, but Eve started to feel down. She didn't want to be a regular at The Black Cat. The food was good and the atmosphere was pleasant, but she longed for the sophistication of her favourite Italian restaurant in Chania. She and David were due a visit there very soon without anybody else. She completely forgot that David wouldn't be a good enough protector with his broken arm. Unfortunately, it would be a while before they could have an evening alone.

★　★　★

To get to Annie and Pete's from The Black Cat, they had to pass by Eve and David's house. As they approached,

Pete noticed there was someone spraying Eve's car!

'There's somebody trying to damage to your car, Eve,' he said, stopping short. 'If we approach quietly, we might be able to catch him.'

Eve, however, had other ideas. She jumped out of the car — followed quickly by David, who forgot all about his broken arm. He just wanted to make sure Eve didn't do anything stupid and get hurt.

They dashed towards her car. Pete got out of his car a moment later and followed them. As she reached her Mercedes Eve noticed the culprit was dressed in black with a balaclava. She grabbed his arm, and then David careered into both of them. He was shoved away, hitting his head on the car. Pete reached them within seconds, wanting to help. Eve was so incensed that someone was trying to destroy her car that she was filled with a strength she didn't realise she had. She almost tore the balaclava off the culprit, desperate to know who had been terrorising her.

Both she and Pete stopped in their tracks, neither able to believe their eyes. It was none other than Betty Jones.

'Betty!' Eve exclaimed. 'I'm stunned. I can't believe it's you. I knew you didn't like me, but you must really hate me!'

When Betty spoke she sounded almost proud. 'Yes, and it's not all I've done. I was the one who ransacked your house and slashed the tyres on your car. And I sent you an anonymous letter — and the dead bird. You deserved all of it! You can't imagine how terrible my life has been since you came to the island. You sail around with your perfect make-up and hair, looking down your nose on the rest of us. I can't bear to think of you with David — he deserves someone better!'

'David, are you listening to this?' Eve asked.

She looked down, but David was out cold.

'Oh no, David needs help!' she exclaimed, bending down. 'See what you've done, Betty.'

'It's not my fault. I would never hurt David!'

'Well, this *is* all your fault. If he doesn't wake up, it will be all due to you.'

Betty looked as if she were about to burst into tears, but Eve didn't care.

By this time Annie had joined them. Like the others, she was shocked to see that the culprit was Betty. How could Betty have been so nasty? Then she noticed that David was lying flat out on the ground.

'Pete, you'll have to call the police — and an ambulance. David's hurt,' Annie exclaimed.

'You and Eve hold onto Betty while I call.'

'I'm hardly going to go anywhere,' Betty mumbled. 'You know I'm to blame.' She turned and glared at Eve. 'And I'd do it all over again.'

Eve was still finding this hard to take

in. What had she done to Betty to make her despise her this much? Eve didn't like her, but she would never do anything to actually harm her.

At that moment, David stirred. Eve let go of Betty and bent down to speak to him.

'David, are you all right? You're making a habit of hitting your head, aren't you?'

'I am, aren't I? I feel OK, but the head does hurt a bit. Who was it, Eve? Did we catch him?'

'Yes, but it's not a him. It's Betty.'

'Betty?' David exclaimed. 'I don't believe it!' He turned to look at her. 'Betty, how could you? I thought you were my friend.'

'I am, David, but you deserve better than Eve.'

'I love Eve and you'll have to accept it. I know you two argue a lot, but Eve's been kind to you. I mean she even invited you to our wedding.'

'You remember that, David?' Eve asked.

'I also remember us dancing the first dance at the reception, but I'm afraid I can't remember much else. I'm sorry, Eve, but still, it's progress.'

'But you said you love me. How can you love me without remembering everything?'

'I don't know, Eve, but spending this time with you . . . well, I've fallen in love with you all over again. I can't imagine life without you, even though you can be difficult and stubborn at times.'

Eve was speechless for once. He loved her! It didn't matter now how long it would take for him to regain his memory fully. He wanted to be with her — despite all her faults — and she couldn't be more delighted.

In the split second that Pete and Annie were looking happily at Eve and David, Betty pushed Annie out of the way and started to make a run for it! She knew she couldn't escape but perhaps she hadn't been able to bear David telling Eve that he loved her.

Pete bounded after Betty and as he grabbed her she punched him in the eye. Pete fell to the ground groaning with pain and Betty started running again. However, Pete managed to get himself up and ran after her. She was no match for his speed and it wasn't long before he came back with her.

'What was the point of that, Betty?' Annie asked. 'We know where you live and I can't see you going on the run.'

Betty burst into tears. 'I've made a mess of everything! And now I'm going to languish in some awful Greek jail. I won't be able to bear it!'

'Perhaps you should have thought about that before you started doing these things to me.'

'It may not have to come to jail,' David said.

'Are you suggesting I don't press charges?' Eve asked, incredulous.

'No, of course not, but the police may take pity on her and just give her a fine and a warning.'

'What, to keep doing these bad things to me?'

'I think Betty's learned her lesson now.'

Eve was not happy. Betty had put her through hell and she should be punished.

'Why don't we all go inside and wait for the police and ambulance?' Annie suggested, hoping to ease the tense atmosphere.

'Good idea,' David agreed.

They all traipsed into Eve's house and went to sit in the lounge.

'I'm so happy you've remembered something else, David,' Eve said, deciding to put Betty's actions out of her mind.

'Yes, it's great news,' Annie put in.

'I feel pretty bad though, Eve,' David said. 'I didn't tell Rose to leave the hospital.'

'You were confused and scared. Anyway, it doesn't matter any more. You didn't remember me so how could you have acted any differently?'

'Yes, but I realise it must have seemed like I was trying to decide between the two of you.'

'And you chose the wrong woman,' Betty said.

'Betty,' David retorted. 'If you haven't got anything nice to say about Eve, then shut up. Anyway, Rose is dead.'

Everyone was shocked by David's harshness. Betty burst into tears again, but nobody went to comfort her.

The room became quiet until Eve piped up with, 'Well, I'm having a Metaxa. Will anyone join me?'

Annie and Pete shook their heads, but David agreed to one.

This whole evening had been surreal. David had remembered something else about them and their journey was uphill from now on. Then they had discovered that Betty was the one terrorising Eve. She was almost seventy and yet she had been able to do so much damage.

Eve took a large gulp of her drink.

She was having trouble processing what had happened. She had to accept that Betty hated her with a vengeance, but now she suddenly felt sorry for her. She wouldn't last five minutes in jail with a bunch of Greek criminals. She didn't even speak more than a couple of words of Greek. However, if no charges were pressed, Betty could do her more harm in the future. She would think that she could get away with it.

Eve was relieved when the doorbell rang and she immediately got up to answer it. Chief Inspector Dimitris Kastrinakis stood there looking a little fed up. There was another officer with him.

'Come in, Chief Inspector. I didn't realise you worked so late.'

'I don't usually, but I was disturbed at home as I am dealing with this case.'

Eve didn't know what to say, so just let the officers in. Entering the lounge, Dimitris spoke to Betty first. 'So, Mrs Jones, you are the one terrorising Ms Masters.'

She nodded. 'Will I go to prison?'

'More than likely. For now, I'll take you to the police station where you can make a statement.'

'Very well, but I don't regret what I've done.'

'It would be more in your favour if you did.'

Betty glowered at Eve. 'What can I say? I hate her and that's a fact.'

Eve looked at David and shook her head. Betty was making things worse for herself.

'As for the rest of you, I will need to take statements. Please come to the police station at ten o'clock tomorrow morning.'

'That's fine,' Eve said. 'However, David may have to go to the hospital tonight. He cracked his head again on the car when we were trying to stop Betty.'

'Did it make him regain his memory?' Dimitris asked, smiling.

'Only a couple of things, but still, we're making progress,' David put in.

'Well, let me know what's happening when you come to the station tomorrow.'

The Chief Inspector told his sergeant to put Betty in the car. She got up, not looking at anyone as she left.

'I feel awful,' Eve said when they had gone. 'How will she survive in jail?'

'That's her problem,' Annie said. Eve was surprised to hear Annie being so harsh. 'I'm sorry, but she did some terrible things. She has to be punished.'

Eve still didn't feel any better. She was surprised that she was actually feeling sorry for Betty.

'I think I should ring Don,' she said.

'Why, Eve? They're divorced,' Pete said.

'I know, but I'm sure he still cares for her. She needs someone to help her through this.'

Everyone was surprised to hear Eve being so charitable, especially after everything Betty had done to her.

'I'm proud of you,' David said. 'I don't know if I would be like you if she had terrorised me.'

'Of course you would. You're the kindest man I know, David.'

Eve and David's eyes met and she felt a shiver travel through her whole body. She would have been elated if she'd have known that he was experiencing the same emotions.

Eve dialled Don's number and got a very sleepy hello at the other end. She told him what had happened and he leapt out of bed.

'I'm going to the police station right now. She can't face this on her own.'

With that he put the phone down and Eve told the others what he had said.

'I told you that he still cares for her,' she said.

Nobody could reply as they were disturbed by another ring of the doorbell. This time it was the paramedics who decided that David should have a night in hospital just to make sure his head injury wasn't critical.

'I'm coming with you,' Eve said.

'No, it's all right,' David replied. 'I'll ring you tomorrow to let you know what's happening. You need a good night's sleep.'

Eve eventually agreed and soon they were back at Annie and Pete's, where she collapsed in a chair in the lounge, and then burst into tears. The evening had been so very stressful and she was glad it was all over.

14

Eve was hoping for a better night's sleep. She didn't know why she had cried that evening — everything was fine now. Her pursuer had been caught and David had told her he loved her.

She had been on edge for such a long time and was at last able to release the tension. How had she got through the past few days without falling apart? She could have lost David forever.

However, she felt relaxed now, even though she wished David was with her and not in the hospital. She had completely forgotten about Joanna Neonakis.

Surprisingly Eve did feel sorry for Betty, despite what she had done. What on earth had been going through her mind to bring up so much hatred? She was glad that Don was giving her support otherwise she was sure that

Betty would crack under the pressure.

As Eve drifted off to sleep, her thoughts turned back to David. Now this was all over, she would be able to move back to her own home as soon as possible, and David could come with her. She was sure he would want to. She wouldn't be a prisoner any more and would be able to go where she wanted without an escort.

She felt herself tingle all over as she dropped off to sleep. She couldn't wait to be completely alone with her husband again.

★   ★   ★

As they drove to the police station the following morning, they stopped at Eve's house. She had asked Annie and Pete to go there as she wanted to have a good look at her car.

It was a shock seeing it in daylight. It was a complete mess and she felt tears welling up. Admittedly it was just a car and she could get it re-sprayed, but she loved it and it upset her to see it looking like this.

Betty had done a pretty good job with her spray can before they had got to her. She was certainly costing Eve a small fortune. But she wasn't that bothered about the money. The main thing that she wanted to know was why Betty had felt the need to be so vindictive.

Eve tried to put all this out of her mind so that she could focus on the day ahead. Luckily David's car was back from the garage, so she could use it to go to the hospital. Annie and Pete had done too much for her already and she didn't want to ask them for a lift again.

'Did you sleep well?' Annie asked Eve as they left her house.

'Surprisingly I did. The best night in ages.'

'Yes, it must be a relief now you know Betty won't have a chance of doing anything else to you,' Pete said.

'I still can't get my head around the fact that she was behind the damage to

227

my home and my car.' Eve replied.

'Us neither,' Annie said. 'She was a bossy woman and she didn't like you, but I didn't think she'd go this far.'

'Her hatred went far beyond what was healthy. I don't think there was much I could have done to stop it.'

'I agree. I feel very sad for her.'

They were all quiet for the rest of the journey and Eve was relieved. She didn't want to keep talking about Betty. She had to give her statement and that would be that. From then on she would only focus on the future.

It wasn't long before they arrived at the police station. Dimitris Kastrinakis was in his office ready to quiz them. Annie went in first, followed by Pete, and then it was Eve's turn.

'Ms Masters, please sit down and tell me in your own words what happened last night.'

'Well, Annie, Pete, David and I were driving back from an evening at The Black Cat, and as we approached my house we saw someone spraying paint on my car. It was Betty Jones. She tried to make a run for it, but Pete caught her.'

'Why do you think she was doing this?'

'She hates me. Why I don't know, except that she is very fond of David. Probably she thinks that nobody is good enough for him. She admitted ransacking my house, slashing the tyres on my car and spraying it. Oh, and she also said that she had sent me both the threatening letter and the dead bird.'

'She's admitted all this to us as well. I was surprised how willing she was to tell us what she had done. She almost seemed proud.'

'What's going to happen to her now?' Eve asked at the end of the interview.

'She has been charged and the case will go to court.'

'Is she in a police cell now?'

'No, her ex-husband posted bail and we have their passports so they can't leave the country.'

'Poor woman,' Eve said.

'You say that after all she did to you?'

'Yes, strangely enough, I do feel sorry for her.'

'It's a very sad case, I must say. I know you probably think you're safe now, but we haven't caught Joanna Neonakis yet. I would still be on my guard, if I were you. You should perhaps continue staying with Mr and Mrs Davies.'

'Oh, I don't think that's necessary,' Eve said almost flippantly. She wasn't going to give up her chance to be alone with her husband. 'Now it's off to the hospital to see David,' she continued. 'Hopefully he'll be out today.'

She wasn't really worried. She thought that Joanna would be trying to get out of the country rather than pursuing her.

'Give Mr Baker my regards, Ms Masters,' the Chief Inspector said. 'Let him know that we need a statement from him when he gets out of hospital. Take care and don't do anything dangerous.'

'I didn't this time, but there were still people after me.'

'Still, as I said . . . I know what you're like.'

There was a time when she would have glared at him for saying this, but today she just smiled sweetly before leaving his office.

Life was good again.

★　★　★

Eve entered the hospital ward and saw Don Jones even before she saw David.

'Don, I didn't expect to see you here,' she said, walking over and shaking his hand.

'I just came to see how David is.'

'I'm so sorry — about Betty, I mean.'

'Don't be. What she did to you was awful.'

'But you posted bail. You obviously must still care for her.'

'I feel responsible, Eve, nothing else. If I hadn't filed for divorce, she might never have been driven to do what she did.'

'What's going to happen to her now?'

'I'll stay with her until the trial. She'll no doubt be sent to jail, but I'll be waiting for her when she gets out.'

'Don, you can't give up your life for her.'

'I don't feel I have any choice. I've never seen her so dispirited. She seemed so in control of herself last night, but when I came down this morning it was obvious that she had been crying. She's trying to put on a brave front, but she's not succeeding. She must be terrified about what's going to happen to her.'

'You do have a choice whether to help Betty or not, Don. You divorced her and you're not responsible for her any more.'

'I have to help her, Eve, I just do. I'm old school you see. Let's leave it at that. I'm sure you two have things to talk about. Goodbye David . . . Eve.'

When he had gone, Eve took David's

hand and then kissed him. She was delighted when he responded. It didn't seem as if he was regretting telling her that he loved her.

However, she was too scared to ask him if he really meant it or if he had spoken the words in the heat of the moment. Perhaps he had just said it to upset Betty?

No, David wouldn't do that. He was too honest and caring and wouldn't deliberately hurt anyone.

'Have the doctors said when you can come home?' she asked instead.

'Yes, hopefully later this morning, after they've done their rounds.'

'Thank goodness for that. I've missed you.'

'Even though I barely remember you?'

'Let's try and forget what's happened,' she said. 'It's been a difficult time for both of us.'

'Eve, I have to tell you something . . . ' David said and then hesitated, a troubled look in his eyes.

She was worried. Was he going to turn around and say that he didn't love her after all? She waited, her heart racing.

'I had another dream last night. Despite Betty being caught, this isn't over. Someone is still after you.'

'Oh David, there can't be a third person who wants me dead! I know I've upset a few people, but they can't all want revenge at the same time. That would be ridiculous!'

'You're probably right, but I'm sorry, I can't dismiss this dream. Don't you remember I dreamed that Betty was in a police cell? Well, she was arrested wasn't she?'

'Yes, I suppose so . . . '

'Joanna Neonakis is still on the run, isn't she?'

'Yes, but I'm sure that I'm the last thing on her mind right now. What was the dream about?'

'You were kidnapped and taken to a place where someone took out a gun. There were two people involved but I couldn't see their faces.'

'What happened next?'

'I woke up, I'm afraid, but I had this horrible feeling that you were in a lot of danger from both of them. I think it was a woman and a man.'

Eve shivered. She had felt so happy driving to the hospital; in fact she had felt she didn't have a care in the world. Now David had brought her back down to earth. His premonitions so far had been so near to the mark that she couldn't just forget about this dream.

However, Eve didn't want to talk about this any more so she changed the subject.

'I was hoping we could go home, to my house, today. I suppose you don't think that it's a very good idea now? But we can't keep staying at Pete and Annie's indefinitely.'

'No, we can't, but I can't protect you at the moment — not with my arm in plaster.'

'But what do we tell Annie and Pete? They've not taken any notice of your dreams and premonitions. They'll wonder why we haven't gone home.'

'You're right I suppose,' David said. 'But with Joanna Neonakis on the run we have the perfect excuse. We'll just tell them that she's still a threat and ask if we can stay until she's caught.'

'If she ever is. She's such a slippery character and she has been able to evade capture many times before.'

'Do you really think she's given up, Eve? Or are you just putting on a brave face?'

'I don't know, I really don't. However, I hate to admit it, but you're right. I will have to be careful. Oh, I don't know when this nightmare will be over — if it ever will be!'

★ ★ ★

Eve drove David back to Annie and Pete's slowly, often looking in her mirror. She couldn't help but remember her journey back from the hospital when she was sure she was being followed. It suddenly crossed her mind that Betty hadn't confessed to this, while she had been more than ready to admit to everything else.

That could so easily mean that someone else really was after her and it could only be Joanna or somebody she'd hired to do the job. She realised there and then that she still wasn't safe and had been too carefree earlier that day.

However, she decided not to discuss this with either David or Annie and Pete. They would make her stay at home all the time and she absolutely refused to be a prisoner.

'You seem miles away, Eve.' David interrupted her thoughts.

'Do I? Sorry. I must concentrate on driving. I don't want either of us ending up back in hospital!'

As they drove through Almerida, she saw Karen and Liz walking along together, and stopped.

'Hi, you two, how are things going?' she called.

'Fine,' Liz said. 'We're having a great time. We've just been to the beach and now we're off for a spot of lunch. Why don't you two join us?'

'I'm afraid we can't at the moment, but we'll definitely catch up before you leave.'

Eve was in no mood for chit-chat at the moment. David's dream was pressing heavily on her mind.

Karen said nothing, but Eve noticed the expression on her face. She looked as if she'd rather be anywhere than with Liz. Eve knew that she was keen on Rick and supposed Liz must be cramping her style.

'How's Rick, Karen?' she asked.

Karen didn't have a chance to answer, not with Liz there.

'Oh, he's fine,' Liz butted in. 'We'll be seeing him for dinner tonight.'

Eve glanced at Karen, who seemed to be on the verge of tears. Eve didn't know what to say. Liz obviously wasn't aware that three can be a crowd.

'Well, as I said we must meet up

again. Perhaps in The Black Cat for a drink. Any idea when you'll be leaving the island?'

'I don't know,' both girls answered in unison.

'Well, you have my mobile number, Karen, so give me a ring.'

She nodded and then Eve and David went on their way.

'Poor Karen,' Eve said to David.

'Why's that?'

'Well, she's smitten with Rick, but Liz won't leave the two of them alone.'

'Perhaps he likes Liz better than Karen, but hasn't got the heart to tell Karen.'

'Oh, I don't think so. I saw him look at Karen at my dinner party. It's obvious he likes her.'

'Well, I suppose you women have intuition where relationships are concerned.'

Eve just smiled and then started thinking of ways to get Liz out of the way so that Rick and Karen would have a chance to get to know each other.

15

By the following day Eve had put Joanna Neonakis to the back of her mind. Having had time to sleep on it, she decided that the chances of Joanna coming after her were pretty remote.

Perhaps she and David could move back home after all. Since he had told her he loved her, she had been dreaming about being able to share the same bed with him again. He hadn't even suggested it while they were staying at Annie and Pete's — which she understood — but a little part of her had hoped he might creep into her room during the night.

Feeling a little restless, Eve decided to go into Chania on her own that day. Annie and Pete were going to Heraklion to meet up with some old friends who had moved there and weren't returning until the following morning, while

David wanted to read his books to see what he had written during his lost years.

Eve didn't want him worrying too much so she told him she was just going to the local shops. To give her more time, she also said that she might pop in to see Karen and Liz. She didn't think she was doing anything wrong with such a little fib. It was for David's own good, after all.

'Eve, we talked about this yesterday. Joanna could still be after you so it's not safe for you to go out on your own. And don't forget my dream.'

'Darling, I'll be very careful. I won't park in some deserted spot where I could be kidnapped!'

David didn't know what to say. He didn't want her going out on her own, but he couldn't keep stopping her. They had to try and live as normal a life as possible and that meant doing their own thing every now and then.

Just at that moment, Eve's mobile rang. It was the Chief Inspector.

'Ms Masters, I have some good news for you. Joanna Neonakis has been apprehended. She is at this moment being taken back to jail.

'Thank goodness!' Eve said. 'I'm now well and truly safe.'

'I still think you should be careful. She might have sent an accomplice after you.'

'She tried that last year and it didn't work. I very much doubt that she'll do it again. After all, she got a longer prison sentence because of what she did, and now it will be increased again because of her escape.'

'Yes, but don't take any unnecessary risks.'

'I won't,' Eve replied and closed the call.

'What's happened?' David asked.

'Joanna has been caught so I'll be safe now.'

'Unless she sends someone else after you.'

'Oh David, do stop worrying. I'll be fine.'

He sighed. Eve could be so difficult. After all, he was only looking out for her, but he had already discovered that she was a very independent person and he had to accept this if he wanted to stay with her.

Eve brushed her lips against David's, sending a ripple of excitement down his spine. She was obviously the right woman for him, despite his memory loss, and he was looking forward to restarting their relationship in their own home. Perhaps they should consider it now that Joanna had been apprehended.

However, he then suddenly changed his mind. Maybe they should wait for a little while. He didn't know if he was reluctant to take this step because he was slightly afraid of being alone with her. He had always been a man to take relationships slowly, and in effect he'd only known Eve for days, not years.

★　★　★

Eve decided that before going into Chania, she would pay a visit to Geoff. She hadn't made any progress in Rose's case having been all wrapped up in her own problems, and she wanted to see if he had heard anything from the police. Perhaps now she would be able to buckle down to solving the case.

Geoff opened the door and let Eve in without saying anything. She noticed he was unshaven and he seemed to smell a bit, but whether it was just from cigarettes or possibly from not bothering to wash, she wasn't sure.

'Come on in. Have you any news for me?'

'I'm sorry. I really haven't made any progress so far.' She avoided telling him that she hadn't paid much notice to Rose's death as of yet. 'But I wanted to ask you a few questions . . . Did Rose have many friends? Or was there someone who had a grudge against her?'

Eve spoke as she was led into the sitting room. She noticed takeaway cartons and empty bottles of beer strewn around the room. There was also a musty smell permeating the air.

'Sorry about the mess.'

'Don't worry about it. You've been under a lot of stress lately.'

She took great care sitting down, moving away a couple of chocolate wrappers and an empty bottle of beer. How could he have made all this mess in just a few days?

'Rose didn't have many friends,' Geoff finally answered. 'She made quite a few when she was with David, but most dropped her when she left him. I always told her they weren't true friends and she was better off without them.'

'Was anyone angry enough with her for anything to the extent that they would take matters into their own hands?'

'I wouldn't have thought so. The only person who would take revenge would be David, but he was in hospital. Anyway, why would he after all these years? And he has you now.'

'As far as I can see nobody has a motive apart from us and I certainly didn't kill her. I suppose it could just have been a random act by some crazy person. These things do happen, don't they?'

'Yes, but how do we prove our innocence to the police? I couldn't bear to rot away in a Greek jail for something I didn't do,' Geoff said.

Eve looked at Geoff and was suddenly in no doubt that he was innocent. He looked as if his whole world had fallen apart.

She paused for a moment and then jumped up.

'Wait, I've just got it! Don't worry Geoff, we'll soon be in the clear.'

'What do you mean?'

'I don't know *who* did it, but I know *why*. I've got to get to the police station right away!'

With that she dashed out of the house, leaving Geoff standing open-mouthed in the room.

Eve ran to her car, but before she could get there, she was grabbed from behind.

She felt something in her back and was sure it was a gun! Her suspicions were confirmed a few moments later.

'Do not struggle or I *will* shoot you.'

Eve relaxed her body. There was no point going against her attacker or she could end up dead. Mind you, that could happen anyway. She walked silently to his car. Eve was pushed in to the back, all the time thinking that she recognised the voice of her kidnapper.

There was someone else sitting in the front of the car. She could see it was a woman and she thought she recognised her hairstyle. As they got on their way, Eve heard the doors click shut. There was no way of escape — not that she'd want to jump out of a moving car anyway. However, there would surely be times when the car would have to stop and she might have had a chance of escape. Eve leaned back. There was no point being uncomfortable — even if this was her last car ride ever.

Then the woman turned around.

'Hello Eve, how nice to see you again.'

'Liz? What the heck!'

'Well, I really fooled you, didn't I?'

'What do you mean? Who on earth are you?'

Liz took off her wig and her glasses, making Eve gasp.

'Sarah Marshall!' she exclaimed. 'You're out of prison already? I mean, you were working for Vera Ryan who tried to kill me — and you broke my arm. But that was only last year. Surely you should have been given a longer jail sentence.'

'I got out early for good behaviour. I can be good if I have to be,' she said putting on her wig and glasses again.

'You've come all the way from Australia to kill me? Did Joanna send you?'

'What do you think?'

'I'm thinking yes, but who are *you?*'

Eve asked the man. 'I recognise your voice.'

The man stopped the car and turned around. Eve gasped again. 'Rick! Why on earth do you want to kill me? I don't even know you.'

'Charles Sheffield sent me. Because of you he can't spend his life with the woman he loves.'

'Joanna, I presume . . . '

'Yes.'

'There's no accounting for taste, I suppose.'

'A bit more respect for Joanna, if you don't mind. Sarah and I met up with her and she introduced us to each other.'

'You know she's been caught, don't you?'

For a moment Eve was sure that Rick looked anxious, but he regained his cool very quickly.

'That's irrelevant. We still intend to do what she asked of us. You've tried to get the better of her once too often.'

'What about Karen? Were you leading her on?'

'Karen? She's insignificant, just a girl who has a crush on me. She'll get over it. She's not involved in any of this.'

'I didn't think for one minute that she was. She seems too nice, but then so did you, Liz . . . sorry, Sarah.'

For a moment Eve felt sorry for Karen, but quickly came back down to earth. Why on earth was she worrying about someone else? She was in real danger, but at that precise moment she felt as cool as a cucumber.

She'd been in worse situations before and had always escaped, so why shouldn't she again? Mind you, thinking about it, she didn't know how she would get out of this situation. Rick seemed as tough as old boots and she didn't think he would wait long to dispose of her.

As Rick started the car up, Eve thought about David. He was probably engrossed in reading his books and wouldn't realise how long she'd been gone. Anyway, what good would it do if he thought that something had happened to her? She had his car because hers was at the garage. He could borrow Annie's, but could he drive with his broken arm? Even if he could, he'd have no idea where to look for her. The same would go for the police.

Suddenly she shivered and the reality of the situation dawned on her. Perhaps there would be no escape this time.

* * *

Geoff looked out of his sitting room window. The car Eve had come in was still there sitting outside his house. Where had she gone? She can't have rushed off without taking her car, could she?

He went outside and looked around. There was no sign of her. She'd been gone for at least half an hour and he suddenly felt afraid for her. She had thought of something connected to

Rose's death, and perhaps the killer already suspected her of knowing the truth. After all, she had solved crimes in the past. Had she been kidnapped with a view to silencing her for good? What on earth had she thought of that had made her disappear?

Geoff went back inside and sat down. He should really go and tell David, but despite the earliness of the day, he'd been drinking and he didn't want to end up in jail for drink driving. He was already in danger of going to prison anyway and he couldn't trust his current luck.

Half an hour later he was still sitting. He hadn't looked out of the window again, hoping that Eve had come back for her car. However, the suspense was killing him and he got up again to have a look.

Her car was still there and a feeling of terror overwhelmed him. He had asked her to help him, but now it looked like she was going to suffer because of it.

Geoff went and sat down again. What was he to do? He didn't have David's phone number so he couldn't call him. Then a thought dawned on him. Perhaps Rose had it on her mobile. Her bag was still on the settee so he got up and went to get it. He was shaking. If she did have David's number, she must have always thought she might go back to him. He didn't want to know, preferring to think of their happier times.

In fact, they had been happy for most of the years they had been together. They had been inseparable until the last couple of months — and it had all been his fault. He had started working all hours, leaving Rose on her own. He had wanted to earn more so they could have a better life, but she had got bored and lonely.

Geoff found Rose's mobile in her bag. Still shaking, he typed in David's name and wasn't surprised when he found it was there.

He took a deep breath and pushed

the call button. It rang and it rang, but David didn't answer. When he closed the call, he decided he had done enough. He'd tried to contact David, but he hadn't replied. He really wasn't obligated to do any more.

★   ★   ★

Meanwhile David was fast asleep.

He had been reading one of his novels, but had dropped off. It wasn't that he was finding it boring, but he wasn't getting much sleep these days. He was worried about having more nightmares and he even became a little scared to go to sleep, not knowing what the next dream could be. On top of this, thoughts of Eve kept flooding his mind and keeping him awake. Just a touch from her sent his head spinning and he couldn't remember a time that he'd felt this way about a woman.

He knew he loved her, but he wanted to remember the times they'd shared. Why wouldn't the memories come back? The doctors had seemed positive about his memory returning, but why was it taking so long? . . .

All of a sudden David woke up with a start.

'Eve's in danger!' he shouted out loud, but there was nobody to hear him. This time he couldn't even remember what the dream had been about. All he knew was that if he didn't find Eve as soon as possible, she could die!

David jumped off the bed, hurting his good arm. What was he to do? Eve was somewhere close by, but he had no idea where. How would he be able to find her? Was she still even in the area? He had a nagging feeling she had been abducted, but by whom he had no idea.

He searched for his phone. Perhaps Eve had tried to ring him and he had slept through it. However, when he looked at his call log, there was only a missed call from Rose's phone. His heart jumped. Rose was dead — so how could she be ringing him?

He pulled himself together, telling himself to not be ridiculous. Tentatively he called Rose's number. Within a few seconds Geoff picked it up.

'David, is that you?'

'Yes, Geoff. What do you want?'

He couldn't help being a little sharp with him. Knowing that he'd stolen his first wife, he couldn't forgive him.

Geoff responded quietly, 'I think something may have happened to Eve.'

'What have you done with her?'

'I haven't done anything with her, David. She came to see me to talk about Rose, but then she rushed off saying she knew why Rose had been killed, but she didn't give me any details.'

'So what makes you think something's happened to her?'

'Well, her car's still outside my house.'

'Her car's in the garage. Oh no — she must have taken mine. I have no way of getting out to look for her.'

'How would you be able to find her?

She could be anywhere. Anyway, you can't drive with a broken arm, can you?'

Geoff was telling him everything he knew already and he was getting more agitated. Why did Annie and Pete choose today to go to Heraklion? If they'd been here, they could have helped him search for Eve. There was only one thing he could do. He didn't want to, but he had no choice.

'Can you help me find her, Geoff?'

Geoff hesitated. The beer he'd had earlier must be out of his system by now. He hadn't had another drink since Eve had visited. A quick cup of coffee and he'd be as right as rain.

'OK David, I'll help you. I don't want you going through what I'm suffering.'

'I'm at Annie and Pete's. You know where?'

'Yes. I'll pick you up as soon as I can.'

★ ★ ★

'You killed Rose, didn't you, Rick?' Eve asked.

'My, my, what a clever woman you are Eve Baker. How did you work that one out?'

'The only people who are suspects in her murder are me and Rose's partner, Geoff. I didn't kill her and Geoff swears he didn't, and I'm inclined to believe him. He seems to be in a right mess. That can only mean that Rose was mistaken for me. That's not very clever is it, Rick? My name is Masters by the way, not Baker.'

'I saw her at the hospital holding your husband's hand. Bet you didn't know that, did you?' he said, grinning. 'They looked like a married couple so when she left, I followed her home. It was too easy. She had no idea she was being followed and didn't even hear me creeping up on her. She'd left the front door unlocked. How stupid can you get? Mind you, it wasn't the most satisfying kill. The woman barely struggled.'

Eve was disgusted by his words.

'And you feel proud of yourself, for killing an innocent woman?'

'I wouldn't go that far. I've already had a good rollicking about my mistake, but I won't shed tears over a stranger.'

Eve suddenly felt sick. This man was a ruthless killer and she had no doubt whatsoever that he wouldn't hesitate for one minute to kill her. She hoped that perhaps Sarah might try and stop him. She knew Sarah and didn't think she was as tough as Rick or Joanna. However, perhaps Sarah wouldn't have a choice in the matter.

'So, what are you going to do with me?'

She dreaded the answer.

'I think you know what's going to happen to you, but we might have a bit of fun first. It was too easy killing that other woman.'

Eve leaned back in her seat. This was probably going to be it. Where was David when she really needed him?

16

David knew that every second counted if they wanted to save Eve's life, and he was beginning to fear they might already be too late and was a little short with Geoff when he finally turned up twenty minutes after their phone call.

'Couldn't you have driven any faster? And it took you long enough to realise that Eve hadn't got in her car,' he said. He paused, realising that Geoff didn't need to help him like this. 'Sorry. I'm on edge. I couldn't bear to lose Eve.'

'Understood. Where do we go?'

'I wish I knew. It might be best to go to the police station and see the Chief Inspector.'

'I don't much want to go there.'

Geoff knew that he wasn't a favourite of the Chief Inspector. He was certain that he still considered him a suspect in Rose's murder.

'Well, suggest something else then,' David snapped impatiently. All he was aware of was that they were wasting time.

'I don't know where to start. We'll go to the police station if you want, but I'll stay in the car.'

David nodded and then they were on their way.

★ ★ ★

'Where are we going now?' Eve asked Rick.

'I haven't decided. You know what, perhaps we should ask for a ransom instead of killing you. What do you reckon, Sarah?'

'Joanna will kill us if we don't get rid of her.'

'We could disappear with the cash. The world's our oyster.'

'I don't know, Rick. It's risky. Joanna has friends all over the place and she doesn't forgive easily.'

'You won't get a lot for me, anyway,' Eve interrupted. 'I'm the one with the money and my accounts are all in my name. David won't be able to get hold of much cash.'

'He's a kept man? That must sting! Don't know if I'd like a woman running my financial affairs.'

'He's fine with it.'

'He'll be a rich man if you die. Doesn't that worry you?'

'David loves me. He would rather have me than a bundle of cash.'

'You so sure of that? He's lost his memory. He might think the money's a better option.'

'David isn't like you, Rick.'

'Come on, Rick,' Sarah intervened. 'I don't know what you're playing at. Joanna wants us to kill Eve, so let's just get on with it.'

'I've got other ideas. If you're not interested, I'll drop you off now. Joanna's not paying us nearly enough to kill Eve.'

'Well, that's probably your fault, since you've already botched this up once.'

Eve listened with interest. They were obviously on different pages. Perhaps this could work in her favour, give her more time to plan an escape.

'Why have you changed your mind?' Sarah asked. 'I just want to get this over and done with.'

'Patience Sarah,' he said. 'We'll talk some more when we get back to the hotel.'

'We're going to your hotel?' Eve asked.

'Yes,' Rick said, 'but don't try any funny business. I have a gun and I'll shoot you if you try to alert anyone.'

Eve sighed. There really seemed to be no way out of this situation.

'OK, Rick,' Sarah said. 'We'll talk some more. I must admit the money does sound appealing.'

'Great, let's go then,' Rick replied.

★   ★   ★

Geoff and David arrived at the police station in no time at all. David rushed in, leaving Geoff in the car. Luckily for him, the Chief Inspector was in his office. David breathed a sigh of relief. Perhaps some action could be taken at last. All he knew was that he had to save Eve, and time was of the essence. He walked straight into the Chief Inspector's office without even bothering to knock.

'Chief Inspector, I think Eve's been abducted!' he blurted out. 'She went to see Geoff in my car because hers is in the garage, and the car is still outside Geoff's house but now Eve is nowhere to be found.'

'Calm down, Mr Baker.'

'How can I be calm with my wife missing? I knew it wasn't all over. Why did I let her go off on her own? I thought she was only going to the shops, but she went to see Geoff instead. Why did she lie?'

'I have no idea. Eve is a law unto herself. We both know that . . . or perhaps you can't remember what she's like?'

'My memory is slowly coming back. I'm sure it won't be long before I'll be able to remember everything. All I know is I'm worried sick about her. Why are we wasting time?'

He couldn't believe the Chief Inspector's attitude. He thought that under that brusque exterior, he was actually a little fond of Eve. Perhaps he'd got it all wrong?

'I'm sorry, Mr Baker. Of course I don't want anything to happen to Ms Masters. But where do you suggest we start? Have you any idea of where she might have been taken — and by whom?'

'I don't know. On the one hand I have a strong feeling her disappearance is connected with Rose's death — but I don't know if Joanna is behind it.'

'What did Geoff say about Eve's visit?'

'Not a lot. He's in his car outside if you want to talk to him.'

'Very well. Let's go.'

As they came out of the police station, Geoff saw them and started to panic. Perhaps the alcohol was still in his system. It didn't even cross his mind that he was doing something stupid — he just instinctively put his foot on the accelerator and sped away!

Dimitris and David watched him, open-mouthed.

'Come on Mr Baker, let's get in my car quickly. He needs to be caught. It now looks very suspicious.'

They rushed over to the car. David had barely put his seat belt on before they were off.

'I can't understand this. Geoff called me. I don't think he would have done anything to Eve going missing and then ring to tell me.'

'It could have been a bluff. After all, he did have a go at her about Rose's murder.'

'Yes, but I still don't think he had anything to do with it. I feel certain Joanna has set this up.'

'You're having an awful lot of feelings about this case, Mr Baker . . . '

David said nothing. The Chief Inspector would never take his premonitions seriously.

As they turned the corner, they screeched to a halt right in front of Geoff's car. It had hit a tree.

The Chief Inspector leapt out of his car and ran over to Geoff's car. Looking inside he saw that Geoff was OK, so he opened the door and asked him to step out of the car.

'Are you all right, Mr Carter?' he asked.

'I think so.'

'Why did you drive away?'

Geoff just shrugged his shoulders.

'Do I smell alcohol on your breath? It's a bit early for drinking, isn't it?'

'I was having a bad day, missing Rose and all the stress of being accused of her murder . . . '

'I'm afraid I'm going to have to breathalyse you, Mr Carter. Would you come over to my car?'

Geoff knew there was no point running so he followed the Chief Inspector to his car and allowed him to breathalyse him.

A few moments later the Chief Inspector said, 'You're very lucky Mr Carter; you're just under the legal limit.'

Geoff breathed a sigh of relief. But even if they didn't put him in jail, there was a big fine and he couldn't afford it, not with Rose's funeral to take care of.

David got out of the car. 'Can we get going soon?' he asked. 'Every minute is precious.'

'Patience, Mr Baker. I have to question Mr Carter first.' He turned and looked at Geoff. 'What did Ms Masters want with you?'

'I don't really know. I think she wanted to know if I had found out anything about Rose's death, but of course I hadn't. Then she suddenly perked up and said it all made suddenly sense and then she rushed out of the house. I don't know if she actually knew *who* had killed Rose, but she seemed to infer that she knew *why*.'

'I wonder what she meant by that?'

'I've no idea, Chief Inspector. Can I go home now? I presume you can help Mr Baker now.'

Before he could answer, David's phone rang.

'David Baker. We have your wife. If you want to see her alive again, we want two hundred thousand euros.'

'What?' David gasped. 'I haven't got access to that sort of money! Anyway, there are capital controls in Greece — you can only take out four hundred and twenty euros a week from your Greek bank account . . . '

'That's not my problem. I will ring you tomorrow and tell you where to bring the money.'

With that the caller closed the call, leaving David stunned.

'They want money, Chief Inspector — two hundred thousand euros, to be exact, and they want it by tomorrow. I can't get hold of that much money! Not even Eve herself would be able to withdraw two hundred thousand euros overnight. A lot of her money is tied up in stocks and shares. It could take days to sort out! What are we going to do, Chief Inspector? They're going to kill her, aren't they?'

'They could be bluffing . . . '

'Not if Joanna Neonakis is behind all of this. Eve told me that Joanna had arranged to have me kidnapped last year, but she only wanted one hundred thousand euros that time. Luckily I was rescued and she didn't get hold of Eve's money.'

'I know. I remember it well. I think the only thing you can do is to stall them in some way when they next call.'

'But what do we do in the meantime? I can't sit around for hours waiting for the phone call.'

'I'm afraid you don't have any choice. We have no idea where she has been taken, none whatsoever. We're at the mercy of her kidnappers. I think that the only option for the moment is to take you home, Mr Baker.'

'I'm still staying with Pete and Annie, so can you drop me off there please?'

'Very well. And do try to keep calm.'

David said nothing. This woman he could hardly remember had made such an impact on him — and he didn't want to lose her.

* * *

At the hotel Eve sat on a chair in Sarah's room. It was a superior room and Eve suspected that Joanna had paid for it. Rick was also in the room and held his gun pointing at her. She thought there was no need for him to do this continually, since there was little chance of her getting an opportunity to escape, not with two of them against just one of her.

Eve had been in similar situations before, but she felt in more danger than she had ever been before. A couple of tears fell down her cheeks and she hoped that her captors hadn't seen them. She didn't want to appear weak.

'You know David isn't going to be able to get enough money to pay that kind of ransom?'

'Then he loses you.'

'I can get the money, although it might take a few days. I have stocks and shares.'

'So you say, but can we believe you? Not to mention that we don't have the time. The longer we hold onto you, the easier it will be for the police to find you. No — it's the money tomorrow or you're dead.'

Eve said nothing. Her mind was whirring. There had to be some way that she could get away from Rick and Sarah, but at the moment she couldn't think of a single one.

Suddenly there was a knock at the door.

'Get in there and don't say a word,' Rick said, shoving Eve into the bathroom.

Sarah went to open the door.

'Karen! What are you doing here?'

'I haven't seen you in a while and I was hoping you were all right. I can't find Rick either.'

'I'm fine,' Sarah snapped.

Karen was shocked by her tone. She had always been so friendly. What was going on? Then she saw a man in the room.

'Is that Rick? I knew it! We were getting on so well until you poked your nose in, Rick!'

'Sorry, but Rick isn't interested in you.' Sarah spoke sharply again.

However, Karen pushed her way past Sarah and into the room. Then all of a sudden, she heard a voice shout out for help.

'Who's that? It came from the bathroom. What are you two up to?'

Karen rushed to the bathroom before Rick or Sarah could stop her. She opened the door and gasped when she saw Eve.

'Eve, what on earth is going on here? Why did you call for help?'

Just as she said this, Rick came up behind her and hit Karen over the head. She collapsed, out cold on the floor. Eve moved towards her, but before she could get to her, Rick had pointed his gun at her yet again.

'Leave her,' Rick barked sharply.

'What are you going to do to her?' Eve asked. 'She's done nothing to you.'

'We have no choice now but to get rid of her.'

'Yes, you *do* have a choice! You can let her go once you're on your way out of the country.'

'Get real, Ms Masters. She'll alert the authorities if we release her, even if it's just before we board a plane. I'm not going to jail.'

'You really are a ruthless killer! You killed Rose in cold blood and don't even regret it! Now you want to kill Karen who's done nothing to you.'

Rick just smiled and it dawned on Eve that he could even be a psychopath with absolutely no feelings and he wouldn't hesitate in killing both of them if he thought that was his only way of escape.

Perhaps she could try to talk to Sarah on her own and get her to persuade Rick to let them go? He could tie them up and leave them in the hotel room. They probably wouldn't be discovered until the following day, but at least they'd still be alive.

Eve looked at Sarah and thought she looked a bit nervous. While she had gone along with Rick about killing Eve, she hadn't banked on having to dispose of Karen as well. She had seemed to like her after all, so perhaps there was hope.

★ ★ ★

David couldn't sleep.

There was no way he would be able to get hold of the money for the kidnappers, but then there was no guarantee that they would release Eve even if the ransom was paid, especially if Joanna was behind it. He knew

Joanna wanted Eve dead.

The Chief Inspector had come up with an idea. They would put blank sheets of paper in a case with actual euros on the top. Perhaps that might fool the kidnappers and he could get Eve back. However, there were pitfalls . . . perhaps the kidnappers would look through the case and see that it wasn't full of money. Then he could be killed as well as Eve!

There had to be some other way to get round this. As the night wore on, David fell into a fitful sleep, but woke suddenly at six in the morning.

'I know where they're going to take Eve to kill her!' he exclaimed. 'And there's someone else with her — a woman. They're going to kill her, too!'

He wished the dream had been clearer. He hadn't been able to see who the other woman was, nor who the kidnappers were, although he could tell that they were a man and a woman.

What was he to do?

He knew the Chief Inspector wouldn't

take his premonition seriously and didn't feel he could tell him — he would be ridiculed. He had to do this on his own! Besides, he needed to be the one who saved his darling Eve.

He remembered more of his dream . . . there was no point in turning up with the fake ransom. The kidnappers would see through it and would then shoot Eve and the other woman.

David had arranged to meet Dimitris at eight that morning, when they were to wait for the phone call arranging the meeting place to hand over the money in exchange for Eve. It was still far too early. He'd have a coffee and a couple of slices of toast to keep his energy up and then he'd be on his way.

The Chief Inspector would be waiting for him later on and would wonder what had happened, but hopefully by that time he would have already rescued Eve.

David went through his dream again . . . the cliff where the kidnappers were taking Eve was well imprinted in his mind. It was somewhere that he and Eve had gone for long walks with Portia. He recalled how steep the cliff was and he knew there were rocks in the sea below. It was an ideal place to get rid of someone, but he wasn't going to let them take Eve away from him that easily.

Against all odds, he had fallen in love with her all over again. To hell with getting his memory back — he wanted to spend the rest of his life with her even if he never regained the past three years of his memories!

* * *

Eve wasn't able to sleep either.

Surprisingly she and Karen had been given the beds while Rick and Sarah sat guarding them. They took turns staying awake.

Eve watched them, hoping they would both fall asleep at the same time, then there might be a chance to get away. On the other hand, she thought

Karen would probably hinder any attempt at an escape as, not surprisingly, she wasn't coping well with the situation.

At least Rick had ordered some food for them that evening, although the meal was mainly meat so Eve couldn't eat most of it. She picked at the salad and chips, but didn't really feel hungry.

The meal felt like The Last Supper. Didn't prisoners on Death Row get a final meal of their choice? What would she choose? she thought flippantly. Something Italian from her favourite restaurant in Chania . . . the ravioli tartufo perhaps, or maybe a curry. A really hot one to take her mind off being shot! A bottle of champagne would also go down a treat. Eve almost laughed out loud at her ridiculous thoughts.

Karen barely ate anything either and she kept sobbing. Eve was surprised that Rick and Sarah ignored her. Eve wanted to help her, but what could she do?

'Try not to cry, Karen, please,' she whispered. 'It will probably annoy Rick.'

'It's all your fault that we're in this mess,' Karen whispered back. 'If you hadn't got involved in all those crimes and upset Joanna Neonakis, Rick and Sarah wouldn't be here now and I could still be having a lovely holiday.'

Eve was a little shocked by Karen's reply. She hadn't wanted any of this. She particularly didn't want Karen to suffer, but in the end she couldn't blame her for her attitude. For once Eve looked at the situation from another person's point of view and what else could Karen think? Deep down, Eve knew this was all her fault. She'd do anything to get Karen out of this mess.

On the other hand, Eve thought that it really wasn't fair. For a change she hadn't interfered in anything this time, but her past had come back to haunt her. If she ever got out of this mess, she promised herself that she would never get involved in another crime again.

Karen finally fell asleep about two in the morning and the sobbing stopped. Eve was relieved.

Rick had started pacing and kept looking at Karen. He was unstable and Eve didn't know what he might be capable of doing!

Eve was relieved when she saw the sun rise, even though it could be her last day on earth.

There had to be something she could do to stop Rick. Or perhaps David and the Chief Inspector had come up with a plan? Yes, she was sure of it. They wouldn't let her die without putting up a fight for her.

17

Dimitris Kastrinakis rang Annie and Pete's doorbell twice, but there was no reply. He tried calling David, but he didn't pick up the phone.

'Damn,' he said to his sergeant. 'David Baker has ignored what I told him. I just know that he's gone to find Eve on his own. For all we know, he's been abducted himself by now.'

'What do we do now, sir?' Stavros asked.

'I have no idea. We don't know where Eve has been taken so how could Mr Baker have any idea where to look for her?'

'Unless the kidnappers called David to arrange the meeting?'

'But he hasn't got the money with him, Stavros. Without it, they'll kill Ms Masters, and probably him too. All I can imagine is that he plans to take out the kidnappers by himself.'

'What, with an arm in a cast?'

'He could just be stupid enough to think he could do it! And then how is he going to be able to drive?'

'Not very easily, sir, but it is possible, I suppose.'

'Come on, Stavros, we know what his car looks like. We'll drive around for a bit and see if we can spot it.'

'Wait a minute, sir,' Stavros said. 'Isn't Mr Baker's car at Mr Carter's house?'

'You're right. Well done, Stavros. But he said that Ms Masters' car is at the garage. Do you think that Mr and Mrs Davies have taken him to find his wife?'

'It's possible, sir. There aren't any cars here.'

'This is not good, Stavros. I dread to think what might happen to all of them.'

* * *

David had remembered that Annie had a car as well as Pete. He was sure she wouldn't mind him borrowing it under the circumstances. He just hoped he wouldn't have an accident. He'd never driven with a broken arm before!

He got in the driver's seat. This was not going to be easy, but thank goodness he had at least broken his left arm. He would try and steer with that arm, while changing gears with his other good arm. It was the first time he thought it was helpful that the Greeks drove on the other side of the road.

David started up the engine and the car moved off slowly, stuttering as it went. Then he stalled it and had to start again. He felt completely out of control of the car and thought that perhaps he was being totally stupid, after all.

Perhaps he should just ring Dimitris and ask him to come to the cliff? However, Dimitris would want to know why he thought that was where the kidnappers would take Eve, and he couldn't tell him that he'd had a premonition!

He could always tell the Chief

Inspector that the kidnappers had called and asked him to come to the cliff — but what if they didn't turn up? No, he was better off doing this on his own. He was sure he would get the hang of driving even with his broken arm.

David was driving very slowly and erratically and a couple of cars overtook him, beeping as they went by. All he hoped was that he didn't come across another police car. They wouldn't understand and he'd probably be arrested. Then what would happen to Eve?

A few minutes later he realised he was almost at the cliff. He was relieved. However, when he arrived there wasn't anybody around.

Could he have got it all wrong? Perhaps this premonition wasn't on the mark.

He got out his phone. Shouldn't the kidnappers have phoned by now to tell him where to meet them? When he looked at his phone he saw that it was switched off! How could he have been so stupid? He started shaking. If they had rung they would have thought that he hadn't been able to get the money. For all he knew, Eve could already be dead!

★   ★   ★

In the hotel Eve was sitting on the bed. She felt a mess and thought that most of her make-up had probably come off by now. She hated going out without her hair and make-up looking perfect. Even if she was going to die, she wanted to look her best!

She almost laughed out loud again. How many people would care what they looked like in such a situation as she was in now?

'Well, I've rung your loving husband twice, Eve, but he hasn't answered. It seems as if he doesn't care about you as much as you thought. Looks like I was right and he's more interested in your money. I have no option now but to get rid of you. Get up, both of you,' Rick snarled.

'Can't we just wait a bit longer?' Sarah asked. 'It's a lot of money so it's probably taking him a while to get it.'

Eve was surprised at Sarah's words. Perhaps she wasn't as keen to kill them as Rick was. If she could get her onside it could be three against one, and then they'd have a chance — even if only a slim one.

If only she could talk to Sarah on her own.

However, Eve did what Rick wanted, pulling Karen up with her.

Karen had started crying again.

'Stop that wailing, or I'll have to shut you up permanently before we leave the hotel!' Rick snarled. 'And that could be a bit messy, so I'd rather not have to do it. All I want is for you to stop crying while we walk down to the car. Do you understand?'

With that he shoved her towards the door.

This made Karen cry even more so

Eve gave her a hug and whispered in her ear that it would all be all right. 'Just do what he says, Karen, please. You're making it worse for us.'

Karen nodded and wiped her eyes. She knew that she had to try and stay strong, but it was so hard. Rick was like a madman and who knew when he could completely snap?

'Right we're going to the car,' Rick said. 'I don't want any funny business because I will shoot you both.'

'What good will that do?' Eve asked. 'Haven't you thought it through? You'll be caught if you shoot either of us in the hotel. There are too many people about.'

'We have two guns. That'll make it easier to get away. It's really up to you two. If you behave, innocent people won't have to die. I have been in situations like this before, you know.'

'I'm sure you have . . . ' Eve murmured.

She dreaded to think what other crimes he had already committed. He certainly was a match for Joanna. Did Charles Sheffield know what evil he had unleashed when he had asked Rick to come to Crete to kill her?

When they were in the car, Eve said, 'Where are you taking us? Why don't you try ringing David again? You never know, he might have got hold of the money by now.'

'That's funny,' Rick replied. 'A little while ago you said that he wouldn't be able to get his hands on two hundred thousand euros.'

So much for trying to stall him. Eve decided her only option now was to keep quiet. She would only annoy Rick more and probably bring on their demise sooner rather than later.

Karen was silent. She hadn't said much at all today, but at least she had stopped crying.

However, Eve was still worried about her. She could freak out again at any time and cause more problems for both of them.

Eve wished she could talk to her

without either Rick or Sarah hearing. Perhaps they could plan a strategy to escape. It needed both of them to be in it, but Eve knew she probably wouldn't be able to trust Karen in her state of mind.

Suddenly Sarah spoke out.

'Do you really think this is a good idea, Rick? Killing them, I mean. Don't you think the ransom money would solve all our problems and set us up for life? I'm sure that Eve herself would be able to get her hands on it, even if David can't.'

'You've changed your tune, haven't you? Yesterday you were all for killing them. We'll still be earning money if we kill them rather than wait for the ransom.'

'Yes, but not nearly as much. You said that yourself yesterday. We can go somewhere to start a new life. The more money we have the better.'

'The money's guaranteed if we kill them. Eve might not get us what we want. She might think we're going to kill her even if she gives us the cash, so why pay up when that prat of a husband of hers can have it all for himself? Look, I'm the boss, so what I say goes.'

'Who made you the boss? You're not even working for Joanna — your boss is Charles Sheffield. Until now he hadn't done anything wrong in his life, so Joanna is the one to watch.'

'Yeah, yeah, whatever,' Rick replied.

However, he knew Karen was right.

Joanna was a ruthless killer and wouldn't hesitate to have him killed if he didn't do what she wanted. She was already angry that he had killed the wrong woman. Yes — he was probably better off killing Eve as Joanna wanted, rather than holding out for the ransom.

However, he was worried about Sarah. Even though she had broken Eve's arm the previous year, he doubted very much if she had it in her to actually kill anyone in cold blood. He had no idea why Joanna had sent her.

No; this was up to him and he was going to make all the decisions.

* * *

Rick stopped the car near a cliff and Eve recognised the area as a place she and David had taken Portia for walks.

Suddenly she shivered. Was Rick intending to throw them over the cliff instead of shooting them? What would be worse? Probably the cliff as it wouldn't be immediate and they would feel the fear as they were falling.

On the other hand, perhaps he just wanted to frighten them. Maybe he was still holding out for the money, despite what he'd said earlier.

Why didn't he ring David again? She couldn't believe he would really give up the chance of so much cash. She didn't want to give him a penny, of course, but if she had to, she would, since her life was at stake.

However, perhaps he really was afraid of Joanna and thought it best to kill them rather than try and escape with a lot more money. It would surprise her if Joanna hadn't already threatened him, and knowing Joanna she would find him if he didn't do what she asked.

The possibilities were endless, but Eve had no time to think any more. The car door opened and Rick dragged her out, followed by Karen.

'Right, move over there you two,'

Karen burst into tears again. Eve had hoped she had got herself under control. She was going to try Rick's patience again.

'Please don't hurt me,' Karen pleaded. 'I won't tell anyone what you've done.'

'As if I could believe that.'

'You can, Rick. Can't you remember the fun we had together? I'd go away with you if you wanted me to. I was falling for you, you know that.'

Eve saw Rick hesitate. Was he actually going to spare Karen's life?

However, a moment later he said simply, 'Shut up, Karen. We hardly know each other and the chances are high that we wouldn't get on. I can't see how we could be compatible. Then what would happen? I'd have to kill you anyway.'

'Oh, but I know that we would. Just give me a chance!' Karen pleaded, desperate now.

'Shut up, I won't listen to any more of this nonsense.'

Karen started sobbing again. Her chance of escape had gone.

Eve thought she'd been a bit stupid. Karen wouldn't last five minutes with Rick. She must hate him now, so how could she contemplate spending her life with him? Mind you, her instinct for survival was still strong so perhaps she wasn't as hopeless a case as Eve had first thought.

'Now, move, you two,' Rick hissed.

'Where to?' Eve asked.

'Don't pretend to be stupid. You know exactly where I want you to go. Right to the crumbling edge of the cliff.'

Eve took a deep breath. She had to do something. It was her last chance, but for the life of her she couldn't think of what to do! If she made a run for it, Rick would surely shoot her.

All of a sudden, Eve saw Sarah fall and there was David!

He had knocked her out with the plaster on his broken arm. Sarah screamed as she fell and Rick turned around. Unfortunately, he was too quick and had his gun pointed straight at David!

Eve stopped dead in her tracks.

If she tried to take down Rick, he could easily shoot her husband. They were at a stalemate.

Eve looked at Sarah, who seemed to be out cold. Now there were three of them against one . . . but could she rely on Karen to do anything constructive?

Nevertheless, she had to do something to save them!

Rick's eyes were flitting between her and David and Eve didn't know if she would be able to catch him off guard.

Then Rick glanced towards Sarah and in that split second Eve pounced on him, knocking him to the ground.

He twisted and attempted to point his gun at her, but David was too fast for him. He flew at him with his plaster cast and smacked him in the face. It only stunned him for a moment, and he was up again. He lunged for David and brought him down.

A tussle started and now it was becoming clear that David was no match for Rick as Eve watched in horror. Would Rick kill her husband with his bare hands?

Then she saw the gun lying on the ground.

She moved towards it, but before she could get hold of it Sarah managed to grab it. She hadn't been out for nearly long enough and now she had two guns at her disposal.

Eve didn't know what to do next. She looked towards Karen, but she was just sitting on the ground with her head in her hands, sobbing.

Meanwhile Rick and David were still fighting and Rick was getting the upper hand. Then suddenly, David managed to hit him again with his plaster and he went out cold.

Unfortunately Sarah came over, pushing Eve in front of her. 'Get up, David,' she said. 'Now, or I'll shoot Eve.'

He knew he didn't have any choice. She was the one with the guns and, looking at her, he didn't think she would hesitate to use them.

Eve, on the other hand, was shocked. She hadn't thought Sarah had this in her, but she had obviously been wrong. She was going to kill both her and David now — and Karen too, probably! She'd get her money from Joanna and would simply disappear.

The Chief Inspector didn't know where they were. Oh, why hadn't David brought Dimitris with him? Yes, she appreciated the fact that David had wanted to save her himself, but she didn't need a dead hero!

'Now what do I do with you three? I'd rather not kill you all if I don't have to, but I don't think I have any choice. I can't wait for you to get me some money, Eve. It could take days and I need to be out of the country today.'

Eve and David looked at each other.

'I love you, Eve,' he said. 'I wish I'd had the time to get to know you all over again.'

'I love you, too. I have done from the first moment I first laid eyes on you.'

'Oh, please . . . enough of this soppy stuff!'

However, just as Sarah said this, the sound of sirens filled the air.

From the look on Sarah's face, Eve was sure she was starting to panic, but she didn't let go of the guns.

Two police cars screeched to a halt and four officers dashed out, all carrying guns.

Eve recognised the Chief Inspector. How had he known where to come?

The officers ran towards Sarah, but she shouted, 'Stop or I'll kill them all!'

'And then what? Are you going to kill all of us, too?' Dimitris said. 'We have guns as well so one thing I can guarantee you is that you too will be dead.'

Sarah stared at them. She knew there was no way out of this, but she didn't want to go to jail again. It was bad enough in Australia. What would it be like in Greece being stuck with a load of people she couldn't speak to or understand?

She started moving back, still holding the guns. She looked towards Rick. He was still out cold — and would he even help her if he wasn't?

'I'd stop if I were you,' Dimitris said.

'Why, so you have an easier shot of me?'

'No,' Dimitris called out. 'Watch out!'

However, it was too late. Sarah stumbled and then was gone. All they could hear was her screaming growing rapidly more distant.

Eve jumped up and rushed to the

edge of the cliff, followed closely by Dimitris and Stavros. They all looked down, but couldn't see any sign of Sarah. There were rocks below so the chances of her surviving were slim.

'She's probably dead, Ms Masters. Our men will scour the waters the best we can, but she could drift anywhere.'

Eve felt sick. It wasn't a nice way to go at all and she even felt a little sorry for her.

Then she looked at the Chief Inspector.

'She was working for Joanna Neonakis. That woman just doesn't want to give up.'

'Her sentence will be increased again. At this rate she'll end up serving life.'

'Not that I want to tell you your job,' Eve said, 'but you need to cuff Rick — that man out cold on the ground. He's a ruthless killer. He admitted to me that he killed Rose, thinking she was me. And what's more, he didn't care one bit that he'd killed the wrong person, an innocent woman.'

Dimitris turned round and looked at Rick.

'Who knocked him out?' he asked.

'David — oh, my goodness! I'd forgotten all about him.' She rushed towards him. His face was looking battered and bruised. 'David, let me help you up. How are you feeling?'

'Sore . . . I expect I'll be black and blue all over by tomorrow,' he said, gazing up at her and trying to smile in spite of his swollen lips. 'But I'd do it all over again to save you, Eve.'

Close to tears, Eve lowered her head to his and kissed his bruised lips as gently as she could.

He flinched a little.

'Sorry, darling. My lips are a bit painful.'

'Yes, I can see that — you're bleeding,' she said, gently wiping away the blood.

They were disturbed by the officers leading Rick away. He had woken up and been cuffed.

Dimitris moved towards Eve and David.

'How did you know we'd be here?' Eve asked.

'Your husband was supposed to meet me this morning to pay the ransom with fake notes. He didn't turn up, but at least he had the good sense to call me later to tell me where he'd be.' He turned to David and asked, 'How did you know that Eve would be here, Mr Baker?'

'Oh, I just had a feeling this was where Rick was taking her . . . '

Dimitris looked at him strangely, but didn't pursue the subject.

Eve smiled. Thank goodness for David's premonitions! But she wondered if they would carry on now that they were safe.

Then Eve looked for Karen, and saw that she was still sitting on the ground a little way off and was sobbing.

'It's all right, Karen,' Eve said. 'Rick has been arrested and Sarah has fallen off the cliff's edge. We're all safe now.'

Karen nodded. 'I'm sorry. I was a blubbering mess. I was horrible to you too, even though you were in the same terrible position as me. I should have tried to remain as calm as you did.'

'Believe me, I wasn't calm inside, Karen, but I was determined not to let Rick and Sarah see how frightened I really was. Mind you, I have had more experience in these sorts of things than you. I've escaped from so many dangerous situations that I stayed hopeful no matter what — and it all paid off in the end.'

'What do you think happened to Liz — or should I say Sarah? Could she have survived? Do you think she managed to swim away?'

'I doubt it. There are too many rocks down there. It was difficult to see from up here what happened. The police will search for her, but she may never be found.'

'Oh. I know I shouldn't be, but I do feel a little sorry for her.'

'Don't be, she would have killed us

all. I truly didn't think she was capable of murder, but when Rick was knocked out by David, she took over his role very easily.'

'I suppose you're right. She really had me fooled. I thought she was lonely and insecure and that was why she kept hanging around me. And to think that I was attracted to Rick! He's a cold-blooded killer and I couldn't see it. He seemed so well-mannered and kind, a real gentleman. He's so good-looking as well . . . what a pity.'

'He had me fooled too, so don't fret about it. What are you going to do now?' Eve asked.

'I'm going to get the first plane out of here. I don't ever want to see Crete again.'

'I understand, but perhaps you'll feel differently later. It really is a beautiful island,' Eve replied. 'I'd better go back and see how David is.'

David was still talking to the Chief Inspector when Eve walked over to them. 'Do you want us to make a statement?' she asked Dimitris.

'This afternoon will be fine, Ms Masters. I think you three deserve a bit of a rest this morning. And you, Mr Baker, should go to the hospital to have yourself looked over.'

'Oh, I'll be fine,' David replied. 'I've had enough of that hospital for a while, Chief Inspector.'

Dimitris shook his head, thinking that David could sometimes be just as stubborn as his wife!

Eve and David said their goodbyes and went to fetch Karen, as they had promised they would take her back to her hotel.

'The Chief Inspector wants us to make statements this afternoon,' Eve told Karen.

'Will I be able to go home afterwards — home to England, that is?'

'Probably, but the police might want you to come back when the case goes to court.'

'So much for me not ever having to come back to Crete,' she groaned.

'You can come and stay with us, if you like.'

Karen smiled for the first time in a long while.

'Really? Thank you. That would be nice.'

Eve smiled too and they all wandered over to where Annie's car stood waiting.

Eve glanced at David's arm in plaster, and decided it was safer if she drove them home.

18

When they got back to Karen's hotel, Eve asked her if she wanted them to stay with her for a while. She had been through a lot and Eve was worried about her, even suspected that she might need counselling, but that would have to wait until she got back home.

'No, Eve. Thank you for asking, but I just want to get into the bath and have a long, hot soak. I'm sure you probably want to do the same. I'll see you later this afternoon, when we have to give our statements.'

'OK, but if you feel depressed and what happened keeps coming back to you, just ring me and we can talk.'

As Eve drove back to Annie and Pete's she asked David how he was feeling.

'My body is really aching now, but I suppose it isn't surprising. I can't remember the last time I was in a fight — probably when I was a kid! I just hope that Rick feels as bad as I do.'

'Hopefully he feels worse — he certainly deserves it! At the least he should have a very sore head. I hope you didn't injure your broken arm hitting him over the head — twice!'

'Actually, it feels better than the rest of me. The plaster cast must have protected it.'

'Are you sure you don't want to go to the hospital to get checked out, darling?'

'No, honestly Eve, I'll be fine. I promise though that if I feel worse, I'll let you know and you can take me to the dreaded hospital.'

'OK, if you're sure,' she said, adding, 'You know, I think Karen's right. A nice long soak in the tub will probably work wonders for both of us.'

'I couldn't agree more,' David said with a sigh.

★ ★ ★

It wasn't long before they were back at Annie and Pete's place and they saw that Pete's car was back in the drive. Eve hoped Annie wouldn't be cross that David had borrowed her car.

Entering the house, they heard Annie shout out, 'We're in the kitchen having coffee. Come and join us.'

When they saw Eve and David, both Annie and Pete gasped.

'What on earth has happened to you two?' Pete asked. 'You look as if you've been through the wars. Sit down.'

'Well, Eve was kidnapped again — this time by Rick and Liz, who's really Sarah Marshall.'

'Then David was a hero and came to save me, despite his broken arm. He borrowed your car, Annie. I hope you don't mind. We didn't crash it!'

'Oh, my goodness, forget about that! I didn't even have any idea it was gone. Just tell us everything that's happened since we've been gone. Start at the beginning and don't leave out any details. I don't know . . . we go away for just one night and you get yourself into trouble again!'

Eve and David both grinned and told their story.

$$\star \quad \star \quad \star$$

The following afternoon Eve and David moved back home. For the first time in a while she felt completely safe. She didn't even believe that Joanna Neonakis would try anything again after all her failed attempts — mind you Eve did wonder if she would tell the police that Rick hadn't been working for her in the hope of getting a lesser sentence. Eve had no doubt that Joanna would put her survival ahead of her love for Charles.

Sarah was more than likely dead so couldn't testify against her, and Charles's sentence would probably be increased. Yes, it would be a long time before Joanna and Charles would be able to start a life together, if indeed they ever would.

David was sitting on the patio when Eve came out with gin and tonics for both of them.

'There you are, darling,' she said. 'I think we deserve these after what we've been through.'

'Yes, it's been awful, but we survived,' he replied, taking Eve's hand. A shiver of pleasure ran up her spine. Perhaps David hadn't got much of his memory back, but he had told her that he loved her. That was more important than anything and she was excited about the future.

'I wonder if the police will be able to recover Sarah's body,' Eve ventured.

'I don't know. She could have been smashed to pieces when she hit the rocks.'

Eve shivered at the thought of it. It could so easily have been any of them. Rick and Sarah could have taken a sick pleasure in pushing them over the cliff rather than shooting them!

She had to forget about it otherwise she would be having nightmares. She was usually good at putting things behind her, but at the moment she kept going through everything that had happened again and again. It had probably been the worst kidnapping she had experienced and she felt lucky to be alive. As a result she told herself firmly that this private sleuthing had to end . . . but even as she thought this she felt a pang of disappointment. It had all been so exciting!

'I don't think I want to go to the cliff again,' David said, breaking into her thoughts. 'I know we used to take Portia there for walks, but it holds bad memories now.'

'You mean, you remember walking there with me and Portia?' Eve exclaimed.

'When I had the dream . . . premonition, whatever you want to call it, I knew I recognised the area and I remembered walking there. What's more, during the night, I remembered the first time we met in The Black Cat. I remembered thinking at the time that you were beautiful, but quite out of my league.'

'Is that why you were so shy with me in the beginning, darling?'

'I couldn't believe you were interested in me.'

'How could I not be? You were the most handsome man in The Black Cat.'

David grinned at her.

'Do you remember anything else, David?'

'Yes, actuallly I do . . . this morning I woke up and remembered Rose leaving me. All the hurt and pain she put me through came flooding back, but I feel closure now. That part of my life is really over. I don't think I'll ever think of her any more.'

'Oh David, you don't know how happy that makes me feel! Rose has been at the back of my mind throughout all of this. I kept thinking that part of you still loved her.'

'No, the only woman I love is you, Eve, and I don't need all of my memories back to know it.'

David reached over and kissed Eve ever so gently — his lips were still a little sore. She shivered again, feeling as she had done in the first few weeks of their relationship. All that excitement was back — not that it had ever really left — but the early days of any relationship were always the most powerful. She felt such a strong desire for David that she wanted to throw all caution to the wind and drag him upstairs! Nevertheless, she held back, wanting him to come to her first.

They sat in silence for a little while, watching the sun set. They both felt comfortable enough with each other to not have to talk.

Portia came and sat by their feet. She was making good progress and each day she seemed a little stronger.

Finally Eve said tentatively, 'You'd better choose which bedroom you want to sleep in. If you don't remember, we have six. Probably too many, but it's handy when we have visitors.'

David was quiet for what felt like a

long moment before he looked at Eve and whispered, 'What's wrong with the one we share?'

Eve couldn't believe her ears! David wanted them to share the same bedroom even though he only had fleeting memories of their life together. Everything was back to normal despite all that they'd been through. She couldn't be happier!

'Well, what do you say, darling?'

For once Eve was lost for words and instead flung her arms around her husband. She had wanted to do this so many times in the past few days, but now she understood that it was completely the right time. At last, David took Eve's hand and took her upstairs . . .

We do hope that you have enjoyed reading this large print book.

Did you know that all of our titles are available for purchase?

We publish a wide range of high quality large print books including:
Romances, Mysteries, Classics
General Fiction
Non Fiction and Westerns

Special interest titles available in large print are:
The Little Oxford Dictionary
Music Book, Song Book
Hymn Book, Service Book

Also available from us courtesy of Oxford University Press:
Young Readers' Dictionary
(large print edition)
Young Readers' Thesaurus
(large print edition)

For further information or a free brochure, please contact us at:
Ulverscroft Large Print Books Ltd.,
The Green, Bradgate Road, Anstey,
Leicester, LE7 7FU, England.
Tel: (00 44) **0116 236 4325**
Fax: (00 44) **0116 234 0205**

Other titles in the
Linford Romance Library:

WINTER GOLD

Sheila Spencer-Smith

Recovering from a bereavement, Katie Robertson finds an advertisement for a temporary job on the Isles of Scilly that involves looking after a housebound elderly lady for a few weeks. Hoping to investigate a possible family connection, she eagerly applies. But the woman's grandson, Rory, objects to her presence and believes she's involved with sabotaging the family flower farm. With an unlikely attraction growing between them, can Katie's suspicion of the real culprit be proved correct, and lead to happiness?

AFRICAN ADVENTURE

Irena Nieslony

Amateur sleuth Eve Masters has just married the man of her dreams, David Baker, on the romantic island of Crete. Now they are heading off on their honeymoon to Tanzania. Eve has promised her new husband not to get involved in any more mysteries — but when one of their safari party is murdered, she can't help but get drawn in. It isn't long before she's in the middle of a very dangerous game . . .

COULD IT BE MURDER?

Charlotte McFall

Last year's May Day celebrations ended in tragedy for Gemma with the mysterious death of her Aunt Clara. Having inherited her aunt's run-down cottage in her childhood village of Wythorne, Gemma moves in, hoping to investigate the death, and is drawn to Brad, the local pub owner. But what she finds instead is a dead body, and a basket of poisonous mushrooms that have put her unsuspecting friend in hospital. Can Gemma get to the bottom of things before she and Brad become the next victims?

THE PLOT THICKENS

Chrissie Loveday

The Archway Players are struggling this year to put a Christmas production together in their seaside Cornish town. Adam, a member of the troupe since he was a teenager, is distracted by Gwen, his would-be girlfriend. While Gwen, a health care worker who lives with and cares for her father, doesn't always have the time she needs for the production — or Adam. And when the lead actor is attacked and put in hospital, it looks as if the show might not go on — unless new ideas are found fast.

TAKE A CHANCE ON US

Angela Britnell

In Nashville, Zac Quinn has been a single father to ten-year-old Harper since his wife left years back. Despite his family's urging, he's determined to avoid dating and a social life of his own until Harper is older . . . Rebecca Tregaskas's life in Cornwall is stuck in a rut. So when her American cousin suggests a temporary house-swap to enable both of them to reevaluate their lives, she goes for it. But tragedy haunts Rebecca's past — and when she falls in love with Zac, it rears its head once more . . .

LOVE STRIKES TWICE

Jill Barry

On a journey to the Scottish harbour town where her grandmother, Cathy, had a love affair that ended in heartbreak many years before, Sarah Barnes can't help but think of how far away her days of strap-handling on the London Tube seem to be. Currently between jobs, she takes one at a local café — and finds herself falling in love with GP Rory McLean. But when Rory turns out to be the grandson of the man Cathy fell in love with, there are rough waters ahead . . .